Orbitsville

Bob Shaw was born in Belfast in 1931 and had a technical education which led to several years' work in structural design offices in Ireland, England and Canada. At the age of twenty-seven he escaped into public relations. Since then he has worked as a journalist, a full-time author and as press officer for an aircraft firm. Married with three children, Bob Shaw's hobbies – apart from writing – are reading, crafts, and 'sitting with my feet up while drinking beer and yarning with kindred spirits'. He sold his first science fiction story to the *New York Post* when he was nineteen, and is now the author of several novels and many short stories. His books include *The Two-Timers, Other Days, Other Eyes, The Palace of Eternity, One Million Tomorrows* and *Tomorrow Lies in Ambush*, all published by Pan.

Orbitsville won the British Science Fiction Award for the best novel of 1975.

Previously published by Bob Shaw in Pan

The Two-Timers
The Palace of Eternity
One Million Tomorrows
Other Days, Other Eyes
Tomorrow Lies in Ambush

Bob Shaw

Orbitsville

Pan Books London and Sydney

First published 1975 by Victor Gollancz Ltd
This edition published 1977 by Pan Books Ltd,
Cavaye Place, London SW10 9PG
© Bob Shaw 1975
ISBN 0 330 25013 2
Printed and bound in Great Britain by
Hunt Barnard Printing Ltd, Aylesbury, Bucks.

one

The President was called Elizabeth, and it was thought by some that the mere coincidence of name had had a profound influence on her life-style. Certainly, she had – since the death of her father – made Starflight House into something which more resembled an historic royal court than the headquarters of a business enterprise. There was a suggestion of neo-Elizabethan ritual, of palace intrigue, of privilege and precedence about the way she ran her trillion-dollar empire. And the touch of antiquity which annoyed Garamond the most – although probably only because it was the one which affected him most – was her insistence on personal interviews with ship commanders before their exploratory missions.

He leaned on a carved stone balustrade and stared, with non-committal grey eyes, at the tiers of descending heated gardens which reached to the Atlantic Ocean four kilometres away. Starflight House capped what had once been a moderate-sized Icelandic hill; now the original contours were completely hidden under a frosting of loggias, terraces and pavilions. From the air it reminded Garamond of a gigantic, vulgar cake. He had been waiting almost two hours, time he would have preferred to spend with his wife and child, and there had been nothing to do but sip pale green drinks and fight to control his dangerous impatience with Elizabeth.

As a successful flickerwing captain he had been in her presence several times, and so his distaste for her was personified, physical. It influenced his attitude more pervasively than did his intellectual unease over the fact that she was the richest person who had ever lived, and so far above the law that she had been known to kill out of sheer petulance. Was it, he had often wondered, because she had the mind of a man that she chose to be an unattractive woman in an age when cosmetic surgery could correct all but the most gross physical defects?

Were her splayed, imperfect teeth and pallid skin the insignia of total authority?

And as he watched the coloured fountains glitter in the stepped perspectives below, Garamond remembered his first visit to Starflight House. He had been about to undertake his third mission command and was still young enough to be self-conscious about the theatrical black uniform. The knowledge that he was entering the special relationship reputed to exist between President Lindstrom and her captains had made him taut and apprehensive, keyed up to meet any demand on his resourcefulness. But nobody in Fleet Command, nor in Admincom, had warned him in advance that Elizabeth gave off a sweet, soupy odour which closed the throat when one was most anxious to speak clearly.

None of his advisers on Starflight House protocol had given him a single clue which would have helped a young man, who had never seen anything but perfection in a female, to conceal his natural reaction to the President. Among his confused impressions, the predominant one had been of an abnormally curved spine at the lower end of which was slung a round, puffy abdomen like that of an insect. Garamond, frozen to attention, had avoided her eyes when she nuzzled the satin cushion of gut against his knuckles during her prolonged formal inspection of his appearance.

As he leaned on the artificially weathered balustrade, he could recall emerging from that first interview with a cool resentment towards the older captains who had told him none of the things which really mattered in personal dealings with the President; and yet – when his own turn came – he had allowed other raw Starflight commanders to go unprepared to the same inauguration. It had been easy to justify his inaction when he considered the possible consequences of explaining to a new captain that the coveted special relationship would involve him in exchanging looks of secret appreciation with Liz Lindstrom when – in the middle of a crowded Admincom flight briefing – she handed him a scrap of paper upon which she, the richest and most powerful human being in the universe, had printed a childish dirty joke. If the time for suicide ever came, Garamond decided, he would choose an easier and pleasanter way . . .

'Captain Garamond,' a man's voice said from close behind him. 'The President sends her compliments.'

Garamond turned and saw the tall, stooped figure of Vice-President Humboldt crossing the terrace towards him. Holding Humboldt's hand was a child of about nine, a sturdy silver-haired boy dressed in pearlized cords. Garamond recognized him as the President's son, Harald, and he nodded silently. The boy nodded in return, his eyes flickering over Garamond's badges and service ribbons.

'I'm sorry you have been kept waiting so long, Captain.' Humboldt cleared his throat delicately to indicate that this was as far as he could go towards expressing views which were not those of Elizabeth. 'Unfortunately, the President cannot disengage from her present commitment for another two hours. She requests you to wait.'

'Then I'll have to wait.' Garamond shrugged and smiled to mask his impatience, even though the tachyonic reports from the weather stations beyond Pluto had predicted that the favourable, ion-rich tide which was sweeping through the Solar System would shortly ebb. He had planned to sail on that tide and boost his ship to lightspeed in the shortest possible time. Now it looked as though he would have to labour up the long gravity slope from Sol with his ship's electromagnetic wings sweeping the vacuum for a meagre harvest of reaction mass.

'Yes. You'll have to wait.'

'Of course, I could always leave – and see the President when I get back.'

Humboldt smiled faintly in appreciation of the joke and glanced down at Harald, making sure the boy's attention was elsewhere before he replied. 'That would never do. I am sure Liz would be so disappointed that she would send a fast ship to bring you back for a special interview.'

'Then I won't put her to that inconvenience,' Garamond said. He knew they had both been referring to a certain Captain

Witsch, a headstrong youngster who had grown restless after waiting two days in Starflight House and had taken off quietly at night without Elizabeth's blessing. He had been brought back in a high-speed interceptor, and his interview with the President must have been a very special one, because no trace of his body had ever been found. Garamond had no way of knowing how apocryphal the story might be – the Starflight fleet which siphoned off Earth's excess population was so huge that one captain could never know all the others – but it was illustrative of certain realities.

'There is a compensation for you, Captain.' Humboldt placed one of his pink-scrubbed hands on Harald's silver head. 'Harald has been showing a renewed interest in the flickerwing fleet lately and has been asking questions on subjects which loosely come under the heading of spaceflight theory and practice. Liz wants you to talk to him about it.'

Garamond looked doubtfully at the boy whose attention seemed absorbed by a group of metal statues further along the terrace. 'Has he any flair for mathematics?'

'He isn't expected to qualify for a master's papers this afternoon.' Humboldt laughed drily. 'Simply encourage his interest, Captain. I know admirals who would give their right arms for such a public token of the President's trust. Now I must return to the board-room.'

'You're leaving me alone with him?'

'Yes – Liz has a high regard for you, Captain Garamond. Is it the responsibility . . . ?'

'No. I've looked after children before now.' Garamond thought of his own six-year-old son who had shaken his fist rather than wave goodbye, expressing his sense of loss and resentment over having a father who left him in answer to greater demands. This extra delay the President had announced meant that he had left home four hours too early, time in which he might have been able to heal the boy's tear-bruised eyes. On top of that, there were the reports of the ion wind failing, fading away to the level of spatial background activity, while he stood uselessly on an ornate terrace and played nursemaid to a child

8

who might be as neurosis-ridden as his mother. Garamond tried to smile as the Vice-President withdrew, but he had a feeling he had not made a convincing job of it.

'Well, Harald,' he said, turning to the silver-and-pearl boy, 'you want to ride a flickerwing, do you?'

Harald examined him coolly. 'Starflight employees of less than Board status usually address me as Master Lindstrom.'

Garamond raised his eyebrows. 'I'll tell you something about space-flying, Harald. Up there the most minor technician is more important than all your Admincom executives put together. Do you understand that, Harald? Harry?' *I'm more of a child than he is,* he thought in amazement.

Unexpectedly, Harald smiled. 'I'm not interested in space-flying.'

'But I thought . . .'

'I told them that because they wanted to hear it, but I don't have to pretend with you, do I?'

'No, you don't have to pretend with me, son. What are we going to do for the next two hours, though?'

'I'd like to run,' Harald said with a sudden eagerness which – in Garamond's mind – restored him to full membership of the brotherhood of small boys.

'You want to *run*?' Garamond managed a genuine smile. 'That's a modest ambition.'

'I'm not allowed to run or climb in case I hurt myself. My mother has forbidden it, and everybody else around here is so afraid of her that they hardly let me blink, but . . .' Harald looked up at Garamond, triumphantly ingenuous, '. . . you're a flickerwing commander.'

Garamond realized belatedly that the boy had been manoeuvring him into a corner from the second they met, but he felt no annoyance. 'That's right – I am. Now let's see how quickly you can make it from here to those statues and back.'

'Right!'

'Well, don't stand around. *Go!*' Garamond watched with a mixture of amusement and concern as Harald set off in a lopsided, clopping run, elbows pumping rapidly. He rounded

9

the bronze statues and returned to Garamond at the same pace, with his eyes shining like lamps.

'Again?'

'As many times as you want.' As Harald resumed his in-efficient expenditure of energy Garamond went back to the stone balustrade of the terrace and stared down across the gardens. In spite of the late afternoon sunshine, the Atlantic was charcoal grey and tendrils of mist from it were wreathing the belvederes and waterfalls in sadness. A lone gull twinkled like a star in its distant flight.

I don't want to go, he thought. *It's as simple as that.*

In the early days he had been sustained by the conviction that he, Vance Garamond, would be the one who would find the third world. But interstellar flight was almost a century old now and Man's empire still included only one habitable planet apart from Earth, and all of Garamond's enthusiasm and certi-tude had achieved nothing. If he could accept that he would never reach a habitable new planet then he would be far better to do as Aileen wanted, to take a commission on the shuttle run and be sure of some time at home every month. Ferrying ship-loads of colonists to Terranova would be dull, but safe and convenient. The ion winds were fairly predictable along that route and the well-established chain of weather stations had eliminated any possibility of being becalmed . . .

'Look at me!'

Garamond turned, for an instant was unable to locate Harald, then saw him perched dangerously high on the shoul-ders of one of the statues. The boy waved eagerly.

'You'd better come down from there.' Garamond tried to find a diplomatic way to hide his concern over the way in which Harald had increased his demands – emotional blackmailers used the same techniques as ordinary criminals – from per-mission to run on the terrace to the right to make risky climbs, thus putting Garamond in a difficult position with the President. Difficult? It occurred to Garamond that his career would be ended if Harald were to so much as sprain an ankle.

'But I'm a *good* climber. Watch.' Harald threw his leg across a patient bronze face as he reached for the statue's upraised arm.

'I know you can climb, but don't go any higher till I get there.' Garamond began to walk towards the statues, moving casually but adding inches to each stride by thrusting from the back foot. His alarm increased. Elizabeth Lindstrom, whose title of President was derived from her inherited ownership of the greatest financial and industrial empire ever known, was the most important person alive. Her son was destined to inherit Starflight from her, to control all construction of starships and all movement between Earth and the one other world available to Man. And he, Vance Garamond, an insignificant flickerwing captain, had put himself in a position where he was almost certain to incur the anger of one or the other.

'Up we go,' Harald called.

'Don't!' Garamond broke into an undisguised run. 'Please, don't.'

He surged forward through maliciously thick air which seemed to congeal around him like resin. Harald laughed delightedly and scrambled towards the upright column of metal which was the statue's arm, but he lost his grip and tilted backwards.

One of his feet lodged momentarily in the sculpted collar, acting as a pivot, turning him upside down. Garamond, trapped in a different continuum, saw the event on a leisurely timescale, like the slow blossoming of a spiral nebula. He saw the first fatal millimetre of daylight open up between Harald's fingers and the metal construction. He saw the boy seemingly hanging in the air, then gathering speed in the fall. He saw and heard the brutal impact with which Harald's head struck the base of the statuary group.

Garamond dropped to his knees beside the small body and knew, on the instant, that Harald was dead. His skull was crushed, driven inwards on the brain.

'You're not a good climber,' Garamond whispered numbly, accusingly, to the immobile face which was still dewed with perspiration. 'You've killed us both. And my family as well.'

11

He stood up and looked towards the entrance of the main building, preparing to face the officials and domestics who would come running. The terrace remained quiet but for the murmur of its fountains. High in the stratosphere an invisible aircraft drew a slow, silent wake across the sky. Each passing second was a massive hammer-blow on the anvil of Garamond's mind, and he had been standing perfectly still for perhaps a minute before accepting that the accident had not been noticed by others.

Breaking out of the stasis, he gathered up Harald's body, marvelling at its lightness, and carried it to a clump of flowering shrubs. The dark green foliage clattered like metal foil as he lowered the dead child into a place of concealment.

Garamond turned his back on Starflight House, and began to run.

two

He had, if he was very lucky, about one hundred minutes.

The figure was arrived at by assuming the President had been precise when she told Garamond to wait an extra two hours. There was a further proviso – that it had been her intention to leave her son alone with him all that time. With the full span of a hundred minutes at his disposal, Garamond decided, he had a chance; but any one of a dozen personal servants had only to go looking for Harald, any one of a thousand visitors had only to notice a bloodstain . . .

The numbers in the game of death were trembling and tumbling behind his eyes as he stepped off the outward bound slideway where it reached the main reception area. His official transport was waiting to take him straight to the shuttle ter-minal at North Field, and – in spite of the risks associated with the driver being in radio contact with Starflight House – that still seemed the quickest and most certain way of reaching his ship. The vast ice-green hall of the concourse was crowded with men and women coming off their afternoon shifts in the surrounding administrative buildings. They seemed relaxed and happy, bemused by the generosity of the lingering sunlight. Garamond swore inwardly as he shouldered through conflicting currents and eddies of people, doing his best to move quickly without attracting attention.

I'm a dead man, he kept thinking in detached wonderment. *No matter what I do, no matter how my luck holds out in the next couple of hours . . . I'm a dead man. And my wife is a dead woman. And my son is a dead child. Even if the ion tide holds strong and fills my wings, we're all dead – because there's no place to hide. There's only one other world, and Elizabeth's ships will be waiting there . . .*

A face turned towards him from the crowd, curiously, and Garamond realized he had made a sound. He smiled – recreating himself in his own image of a successful flickerwing captain, clothed in the black-and-silver which was symbolic of star oceans – and the face slid away, satisfied that it had made a mistake in locating the source of the despairing murmur. Garamond gnawed his lip while he covered the remaining distance to his transport which was stacked in one of the reserved magazines near the concourse. The sharp-eyed middle-aged driver saw him approaching, and had the vehicle brought up to ground level by the time Garamond reached the silo.

'Thanks.' Garamond answered the man's salute, grateful for the small saving in time, and got inside the upholstered shell.

'I thought you'd be in a hurry, sir.' The driver's eyes stared knowingly at him from the rear view mirror.

'Oh?' Garamond controlled a spasm of unreasonable fear – this was not the way his arrest would come about. He eyed the back of the driver's neck which was ruddy, deeply creased and had a number of long-established blackheads.

'Yes, sir. All the Starflight commanders are in a hurry to reach the field today. The weather reports aren't good, I hear.'

Garamond nodded and tried to look at ease as the vehicle surged forward with a barely perceptible whine from its magnetic engines. 'I think I'll catch the tide,' he said evenly. 'At least, I hope so – my family are coming to see me off.'

The driver's narrow face showed some surprise. 'I thought you were going direct . . .'

'A slight change of plan – we're calling for my wife and son. You remember the address?'

'Yes, sir. I have it here.'

'Good. Get there as quickly as you can.' With a casual movement Garamond broke the audio connection between the vehicle's two compartments and picked up the nearest communicator set. He punched in his home code and held the instrument steady with his knees while he waited for the screen to come to life and show that his call had been accepted. Supposing Aileen and Chris had gone out? The boy had been upset – again Garamond remembered him shaking his fist instead of waving goodbye, expressing in the slight change of gesture all the emotions which racked his small frame – and Aileen could have taken him away for an afternoon of distraction and appeasement. If that were the case . . .

'Vance!' Aileen's face crystallized in miniature between his hands. 'I was sure you'd gone. Where are you?'

'I'm on my way back to the house, be there in ten minutes.'

'Back here? But . . .'

'Something has happened, Aileen. I'm bringing you and Chris with me to the field. Is he there?'

'He's out on the patio. But, *Vance*, you never let us see you off.'

'I . . .' Garamond hesitated, and decided it could be better all round if his wife were to be kept in ignorance at this stage. 'I've changed my mind about some things. Now, get Chris ready to leave the house as soon as I get there.'

Aileen raised her shoulders uncertainly. 'Vance, do you think it's the best thing for him? I mean you've been away from the house for three hours and he's just begun to get over his first reactions – now you're going to put him through it all again.'

'I told you something has come up.' *How many pet dogs,* Garamond asked himself, *did I see around the Presidential suite this afternoon? Five? Six?*

'What has come up?'

'I'll explain later.' *At what range can a dog scent a corpse? Liz's brood of pets could be the biggest threat of all.* 'Please get Chris ready.'

Aileen shook her head slightly. 'I'm sorry, Vance, but I don't . . .'

'Aileen!' Garamond deliberately allowed an edge of panic to show in his voice, using it to penetrate the separate universe of normalcy in which his wife still existed. 'I can't explain it now, but you and Chris must be ready to come to the field with me within the next few minutes. Don't argue any more, just do what I'm asking.'

He broke the connection and forced himself to sit back, wondering if he had already said too much for the benefit of any communications snoops who could be monitoring the public band. The car was travelling west on the main Akranes autolink, surging irregularly as it jockeyed for position in the traffic. It occurred to Garamond that the driver's performance was not as good as it had been on the way out to Starflight House, perhaps through lack of concentration. On an impulse he reconnected the vehicle's intercom.

'. . . at his home,' the driver was saying. 'Expect to reach North Field in about twenty minutes.'

Garamond cleared his throat. 'What are you doing?'

'Reporting in, sir.'

'Why?'

'Standing orders. All the fleet drivers keep Starflight Centradata informed about their movements.'

'What did you tell them?'

'Sir?'

'What did you say about my movements?'

The driver's shoulders stirred uneasily, causing his Starflight sunburst emblems to blink redly with reflected light. 'I just said you decided to pick up your family on the way to North Field.'

15

'Don't make any further reports.'

'Sir?'

'As a captain in the Starflight Exploratory Arm I think I can make my way around this part of Iceland without a nursemaid.'

'I'm sorry, but...'

'Just drive the car.' Garamond fought to control the unreasoning anger he felt against the man in front. 'And go faster.'

'Yes, sir.' The creases in the driver's weatherbeaten neck deepened as he hunched over the wheel.

Garamond made himself sit quietly, with closed eyes, motionless except for a slight rubbing of his palms against his knees which failed completely to remove the perspiration. He tried to visualize what was happening back on the hill. Was the routine of Elizabeth's court proceeding as on any other afternoon, with the boards and committees and tribunals deliberating in the pillared halls, and the President moving among them, complacently deflecting and vibrating the webstrands of empire with her very presence? Or had someone begun to notice Harald's absence? And his own? He opened his eyes and gazed sombrely at the unrolling scenery outside the car. The umbra of commercial buildings which extended for several kilometres around Starflight House was giving way to the first of the company-owned residential developments. As an S.E.A. commander, Garamond had been entitled to one of the 'choice' locations, which in Starflight usage tended to mean closest to Elizabeth's elevated palace. At quiet moments on the bridge of his ship Garamond had often thought about how the sheer massiveness of her power had locally deformed the structure of language in exactly the same way as a giant sun was able to twist space around itself so that captive worlds, though believing themselves to be travelling in straight lines, were held in orbit. In the present instance, however, he was satisfied with the physics of Elizabeth's gravitation because it meant that his home was midway between Starflight House and the North Field, and he was losing the minimum of time in collecting his family.

Even before the vehicle had halted outside the pyramidical

block of apartments, Garamond had the door open and was walking quickly to the elevator. He stepped out of it on the third floor, went to his own door and let himself in. The familiar, homely surroundings seemed to crowd in on him for an instant, creating a new sense of shock over the fact that life as he knew it had ended. For a moment he felt like a ghost, visiting scenes to which he was no longer relevant.

'What's the matter, Vance?' Aileen emerged from a bed-room, dressed as always in taut colourful silks. Her plump, brown-skinned face and dark eyes showed concern.

'I'll explain later.' He put his arms around her and held her for a second. 'Where's Chris?'

'Here I am, Daddy!' The boy came running and swarmed up Garamond like a small animal, clinging with all four limbs. 'You came back.'

'Come on, son – we're going to the field.' Garamond held Chris above his head and shook him, imitating a start-of-vacation gesture, then handed the child to his wife. It had been the second time within the hour that he had picked up a light, childish body. 'The car's waiting for us. You take Chris down to it and I'll follow in a second.'

'You still haven't told me what this is all about.'

'Later, *later*!' Garamond decided that if he were stopped before the shuttle got off the ground there might still be a faint chance for Aileen and the boy if she could truthfully swear she had no idea what had been going on. He pushed her out into the corridor, then strode back into the apartment's general storage area which was hidden by a free-floating screen of vari-coloured luminosity. It took him only a few seconds to open the box containing his old target pistol and to fill an ammunition clip. The long-barrelled, saw-handled pistol snagged the material of his uniform as he thrust it out of sight in his jacket. Acutely conscious of the weighty bulge under his left arm, he ran back through the living space. On an impulse he snatched an orna-ment – a solid gold snail with ruby eyes – from a shelf, and went out into the corridor. Aileen was holding the elevator door open with one hand and trying to control Chris with the other.

'Let's go,' Garamond said cheerfully, above the deafening ratchets and escapement of the clock behind his eyes. He closed the elevator door and pressed the 'DOWN' button. At ground level Chris darted ahead through the long entrance hall and scrambled into the waiting vehicle. There were few people about, and none that Garamond could identify as neighbours, but he dared not risk running and the act of walking normally brought a cool sheen to his forehead. The driver gave Aileen a grudging salute and held the car door open while she got in. Garamond sat down opposite his wife in the rear of the vehicle and, when it had moved off, manufactured a smile for her.

She shook her dark head impatiently. 'Now will you tell me what's happening?'

'You're coming to see me off, that's all.' Garamond glanced at Chris, who was kneeling at the rear window, apparently absorbed in the receding view. 'Chris should enjoy it.'

'But you said it was important.'

'It was important for me to spend a little extra time with you and Chris.'

Aileen looked baffled. 'What did you bring from the apartment?'

'Nothing.' Garamond moved his left shoulder slightly to conceal the bulge made by the pistol.

'But I can see it.' She leaned forward, caught his hand and opened his fingers, revealing the gold snail. It was a gift he had bought Aileen on their honeymoon and he realized belatedly that the reason he had snatched it was that the little ornament was the symbolical cornerstone of their home. Aileen's eyes widened briefly and she turned her head away, making an abrupt withdrawal. Garamond closed his eyes, wondering what his wife's intuition had told her, wondering how many minutes he had left.

*

At that moment, a minor official on the domestic staff of Starflight House was moving uncertainly through the contrived Italian Renaissance atmosphere of the carved hill. His name was Carlos Pennario and he was holding leads to which were attached two of the President's favourite spaniels. The doubts which plagued his mind were caused by the curious behaviour of the dogs, coupled with certain facts about his conditions of employment. Both animals, their long ears flapping audibly with excitement, were pulling him towards a section of the shady terrace which ringed the hill just at the executive and Presidential levels. Pennario, who was naturally inquisitive, had never seen the spaniels behave in this way before and he was tempted to give them their heads – but, as a Grade 4 employee, he was not permitted to ascend to the executive levels. In normal circumstances such considerations would not have held him back for long, but only two days earlier he had fallen foul of his immediate boss, a gnome-like Scot called Arthur Kemp, and had been promised demotion next time he put a foot wrong.

Pennario held on to the snuffling, straining dogs while he gazed towards a group of statues which shone like red gold in the dying sunlight. A tall, hard-looking man in the black uniform of a flickerwing captain had been leaning on the stone balustrade near the statues a little earlier in the afternoon. The moody captain seemed to have departed and there was nobody else visible on the terrace, yet the spaniels were going crazy trying to get up there. It was not a world-shaking mystery, but to Pennario it represented an intriguing diversion from the utter boredom of his job.

He hesitated, scanning the slopes above, then allowed the spaniels to pull him up the broad shallow steps to the terrace, their feet scrabbling on the smooth stone. Once on the upper level, the dogs headed straight for the base on which the bronze figures stood, then with low whines burrowed into the shrubbery behind.

Pennario leaned over them, parted the dark green leaves with his free arm, and looked down into the cave-like dimness.

*

They needed another thirty minutes, Garamond decided. If the discovery of Harald's body did not take place within that time he and his family would be clear of the atmosphere on one of the S.E.A. shuttles, before the alarm could be broadcast. They would not be out of immediate danger but the ship lying in polar orbit, the *Bissendorf*, was his own private territory, a small enclave in which the laws of the Elizabethan universe did not hold full sway. Up there she could still destroy him, and eventually would, but it would be more difficult than on Earth where at a word she could mobilize ten thousand men against him.

'I need to go to the toilet,' Chris announced, turning from the rear window with an apologetic expression on his round face. He pummelled his abdomen as if to punish it for the intervention.

'You can wait till we reach the field.' Aileen pulled him down on to her knee and enclosed him with smooth brown arms.

A sense of unreality stole over Garamond as he watched his wife and son. Both were wearing lightweight indoor clothing and, of course, had no other belongings with them. It was incredible, unthinkable that – dressed as they were and so unprepared – they should be snatched from their natural ambience of sunlight and warm breezes, sheltering walls and quiet gardens, and that they should be projected into the deadliness of the space between the stars. The air in the car seemed to thin down abruptly, forcing Garamond to take deep breaths. He gazed at the diorama of buildings and foliage beyond the car windows, trying to think about his movements for the next vital half-hour, but his mind refused to work constructively. His thoughts lapsed into a fugue, a recycling of images and shocked sensory fragments. He watched for the hundredth time as the fatal millimetres of daylight opened between Harald's silhouette and the uncomprehending metal of the statue. And the boy's body had been so *light*. Almost as light as Chris. How could a package contain all the bone and blood and muscle and organs necessary to support life, and yet be so light? So insubstantial that a fall of three or four metres . . .

'Look, Dad!' Chris moved within the organic basketwork of his mother's arms. 'There's the field. Can we go on to your shuttle?'

'I'll try to arrange it.' Garamond stared through the wavering blur of the North Field's perimeter fence, wondering if he would see any signs of unusual activity.

*

Carlos Pennario allowed the shrubs to spring together again and, for the first time since his youth, he crossed himself.

He backed away from what he had seen, dragging the frantic dogs with him, and looked around for help. There was nobody in sight. He opened his mouth with the intention of shouting at the top of his voice, of unburdening his dismay on the sleepy air, then several thoughts occurred to him almost at once. Pennario had seen Elizabeth Lindstrom only a few times, and always at a distance, but he had heard many stories told in the night-time quietness of the staff dormitory. He would have given a year's wages rather than be brought before her with the news that he had allowed one of her spaniels to choke on a chicken bone.

Now he was almost in the position of having to face Elizabeth in person and describe his part in the finding of her son's corpse.

Pennario tried to imagine what the President might do to the bringer of such news before she regained whatever slight measure of self-control she was supposed to have . . .

Then there was the matter of his superior, Arthur Kemp. Pennario had no right to be on the terrace in the first place, and to a man like Kemp that one transgression would be suggestive, would be *proof*, of others. He had no idea what had happened to the dead boy, but he knew the way Kemp's mind worked. Assuming that Pennario lived long enough to undergo an investigation, Kemp would swear to anything to avoid any association with guilt.

The realization that he was in mortal danger stimulated Pennario into decisive action. He knelt, gathered the spaniels into his arms and walked quickly down the steps to the lower levels. Shocked and afraid though he was, his mind retained those qualities which had lifted him successfully from near-starvation in Mexico to one of the few places in the world where there was enough air for a man to breathe. Locked away in his memory was a comprehensive timetable of Kemp's daily movements in and around Starflight House, and according to that schedule the acidulous little Scot would shortly be making his final inspection tour of the afternoon. The tour usually took him along the circular terrace, past the shrubbery in which Harald's body was hidden – and how much better it would have been if Domestic Supervisor Kemp had made the fearful discovery.

Pennario kept slanting downwards across the hill until he had reached the lowest point from which he could still see a sector of the upper terrace and gauge Kemp's progress along it. He moved into the shade of an ivy-covered loggia, set the dogs on the ground and pretended to be busy adjusting their silver collars. The excited animals fought to get free, but Pennario held them firmly in check.

It was important to him that they did not make their predictable dash to the terrace until Kemp was in exactly the right place to become involved with their discovery. Pennario glanced at his watch.

'Any minute now, my little friends,' he whispered. 'Any minute now.'

*

In contrast to what Garamond had feared, the field seemed quieter than usual, its broad expanses of ferrocrete mellowed to the semblance of sand by the fleeting sunlight. Low on the western horizon a complexity of small clouds was assembled like a fabulous army, their helmets and crests glowing with fire, and several vaporous banners reached towards the zenith in deepening pink. As the car drew to a halt outside the S.E.A. complex Garamond shielded his eyes, looked towards his assigned take-off point and saw the squat outline of the waiting shuttle. Its door was open and the boarding steps were in place. The sight filled him with a powerful urge to drive to the shuttle, get Aileen and Chris on board, and blast off towards safety. There were certain pre-flight formalities, however, and take off without observing them could lead to the wrong sort of radio message being beamed up to the *Bissendorf* ahead of him. He pushed a heavy lock of hair away from his forehead and smiled for the benefit of Aileen and the driver.

'Some papers to sign in here, then we'll take the slidewalk out to the shuttle,' he said easily as he opened the car door and got out.

'I thought Chris and I'd be going up to the observation floor,' Aileen replied, not moving from her seat.

'There's no fun in that, is there, Chris?' Garamond lifted the boy off Aileen's knee and set him down on the steps of the S.E.A. building. 'What's the point in having a Dad who's a flickerwing captain if you can't get a few extra privileges? You'd like to look right inside the shuttle, wouldn't you?'

'Yes, Dad.' Chris nodded, but with a curious reserve, as if he had sensed something of Aileen's unease.

'Of course, you would.' Garamond took Aileen's hand, drew her out of the car and slammed the door. 'That's all, driver – we can look after ourselves from here on.' The driver glanced back once, without speaking, and accelerated away towards the transport pool.

Aileen caught Garamond's arm. 'We're alone now, Vance. What's . . . ?'

'Now you two stand right here on these steps and don't move till I come out. This won't take long.' Garamond sprinted up the steps, returned the salutes of the guards at the top, and hurried towards the S.E.A. Preflight Centre. The large square room looked unfamiliar when he entered, as though seen through the eyes of the young Vance Garamond who had been so impressed by it at the beginning of his first exploratory command. He ran to the long desk and slapped down his flight authorization documents.

'You're late, Captain Garamond,' commented a heavily built ex-quartermaster called Herschell, who habitually addressed outgoing captains with a note of rueful challenge which was meant to remind them he had not always held a desk job.

'I know – I couldn't get away from Liz.' Garamond seized a stylus and began scribbling his name on various papers as they were fed to him.

'Like that, was it? She couldn't let you go?'

'That's the way it was.'

'Pity. I'd say you've missed the tide.' Herschell's pink square face was sympathetic.

'Oh?'

'Yeah – look at the map.' Herschell pointed up at the vast solid-image chart of the Solar System and surrounding volume of interstellar space which floated below the domed ceiling. The solar wind, represented by yellow radiance, was as strong as ever and Garamond saw the healthy, bow-shaped shock wave on the sunward side of Earth, where the current impacted on the planet's geomagnetic field. Data on the inner spirals of the solar wind, however, were of interest only to interplanetary travellers – and his concern was with the ion count at the edge of the system and beyond. Garamond searched for the great arc of the shock front near the orbit of Uranus where the solar wind, attenuated by distance from Sol, built up pressure against the magnetic field of the galaxy. For a moment he saw nothing, then his eyes picked out an almost invisible amber halo, so faint that it could have represented nothing more than a tenth of an ion per cubic centimetre. He had rarely seen the front looking so feeble. It appeared that the sun was in a niggardly mood, unwilling to assist his ship far up the long gravity slope to interstellar space.

Garamond shifted his attention to the broad straggling bands of green, blue and red which plotted the galactic tides of fast-moving corpuscles as they swept across the entire region. These vagrant sprays of energetic particles and their movements meant as much to him as wind, wave and tide had to the skipper of a transoceanic sailing ship. All spacecraft built by Starflight – which meant all spacecraft built on Earth – employed intense magnetic fields to sweep up interstellar atomic debris for use as reaction mass. The system made it possible to conduct deep-space voyages in ships weighing as little as ten thousand tons, as against the million tons which would have been the minimum for a vessel which had to transport its own reaction mass.

Flickerwing ships had their own disadvantages in that their efficiency was subject to spatial 'weather'. The ideal mission profile was for a ship to accelerate steadily to the midpoint of its journey and decelerate at the same rate for the remainder of the trip, but where the harvest of charged particles was poor the rate of speed-change fell off. If that occurred in the first half of a voyage it meant that the vessel took longer than planned to reach destination; if it occurred in the second half the ship was deprived of the means to discard velocity and would storm through its target system at unmanageable speed, sometimes not coming to a halt until it had overshot by light-days. It was to minimize such uncertainties that Starflight maintained chains of automatic sensor stations whose reports, transmitted by low-energy tachyon beams, were continuously fed into weather charts.

And, as Garamond immediately saw, the conditions in which he hoped to achieve high-speed flight were freakishly, damnably bad.

More than half the volume of space covered by the map seemed entirely void of corpuscular flux, and such fronts as were visible in the remainder were fleeing away to the galactic south. Only one wisp of useful density – possibly the result of heavy particles entangling themselves in an irregularity in the interplanetary magnetic field – reached as far back as the orbit of Mars, and even that was withdrawing at speed.

'I've got to get out of here,' Garamond said simply.

Herschell handed him the traditional leather briefcase containing the flight authorization documents. 'Why don't you take off out of it, Captain? The *Bissendorf* is ready to travel, and I can sign the rest of this stuff by proxy.'

'Thanks.' Garamond took the briefcase and ran for the door.

'Don't let that ole bit of dust get away,' Herschell called after him, one flickerwing man to another. 'Scoop it up good.'

Garamond sprinted along the entrance hall, relieved at being able to respond openly to his growing sense of urgency. The sight of ships' commanders running for the slidewalks was quite a common one in the S.E.A. Centre when the weather was breaking. He found Aileen and Chris on the front steps, exactly where he had left them. Aileen was looking tired and worried, and holding the boy close to her side.

'All clear,' he said. He caught Aileen by the upper arm and urged her towards the slidewalk tunnel. She fell in step with him readily enough but he could sense her mounting unease. 'Let's go!'

'Where to, Vance?' She spoke quietly, but he understood she was asking him the big question, communicating on a treasured personal level which neither of them would ever willingly choose to disrespect. He glanced down at Chris. They were on the slidewalk now, slanting down into the tunnel and the boy seemed fascinated by the softly tremoring ride.

'When I was waiting to see the President this afternoon I was asked to take care of young Harald Lindstrom for an hour . . .' The enormity of what he had to say stilled the words in his throat.

'What happened, Vance?'

'I . . . I didn't take care of him very well. He fell and killed himself.'

'Oh!' The colour seeped away from beneath the tan of Aileen's face. 'But how did you get away from . . . ?'

'Nobody saw him fall. I hid the body in some bushes.'

'And now we're running?'

'As fast as we can go, sweet.'

Aileen put her hand on Chris's shoulder. 'Do you think Elizabeth would . . . ?'

'Automatically. Instinctively. There'd be no way for her *not* to do it.'

Aileen's chin puckered as she fought to control the muscles around her mouth. 'Oh, Vance! This is terrible. Chris and I can't go up there.'

'You can, and you're going to.' Garamond put his arm around Aileen and was alarmed when she sagged against him with her full weight. He put his mouth close to her ear. 'I can't do this alone. I need your help to get Chris away from here.'

She straightened with difficulty. 'I'll try. Lots of women go to Terranova, don't they?'

'That's better.' Garamond gave her arm an encouraging squeeze and wondered if she really believed they could go to the one other human-inhabited Starflight-dominated world in the universe. 'Now, we're almost at the end of the tunnel. When we get up the ramp, pick Chris up and walk straight on to the shuttle with him as if it was a school bus. I'll be right behind you blocking the view of anybody who happens to be watching from the tower.'

'What will the other people say?'

'There'll be nobody else on the shuttle apart from the pilots, and I'll talk to them.'

'But won't the pilots object when they see us on board?'

'The pilots won't say a word,' Garamond promised, slipping his hand inside his jacket.

*

At Starflight House, high on the sculpted hill, the first man had already died.

Domestic Supervisor Arthur Kemp had been planning his evening meal when the two spaniels bounded past him and darted into the shrubbery on the long terrace. He paused, eyed them curiously, then pushed the screen of foliage aside. The light was beginning to fail, and Kemp – who came from the comparatively uncrowded, unpolluted, unravaged north of Scotland – lacked Carlos Pennario's sure instinct concerning matters of violent and premature death. He dragged Harald's body into the open, stared for a long moment at the black deltas of blood which ran from nostrils and ears, and began to scream into his wrist communicator.

Elizabeth Lindstrom was on the terrace within two minutes.

She would not allow anybody to touch her son's remains and, as the staff could not simply walk away, there formed a dense knot of people at the centre of which Elizabeth set up her court of enquiry. Standing over the small body, satin-covered abdomen glowing like a giant pearl, she spoke in a controlled manner at first. Only the Council members who knew her well understood the implications of the steadily rising inflexions in her voice, or of the way she had begun to finger a certain ruby ring on her right hand. These men, obliged by rank to remain close to the President, nevertheless tried to alter their positions subtly so that they were shielded by the bodies of other men, who in turn sensed their peril and acted accordingly. The result was that the circle around Elizabeth grew steadily larger and its surface tension increased.

It was into this arena of fear that Domestic Supervisor Kemp was thrust to give his testimony. He answered several of her questions with something approaching composure, but his voice faltered when – after he too had confirmed Captain Garamond's abrupt departure from the terrace – Elizabeth began pulling out her own hair in slow, methodical handfuls. For an endless minute the soft ripping of her scalp was the only sound on the terrace.

Kemp endured it for as long as was humanly possible, then turned to run. Elizabeth exploded him with the laser burst from her ring, and was twisting blindly to hose the others with its fading energies when her senior physician, risking his own life, fired a cloud of sedative drugs into the distended veins of her neck. The President lost consciousness almost as once, but she had time to utter three words:

'Bring me Garamond.'

three

Garamond crowded on to the stubby shuttlecraft with Aileen and looked forward. The door between the crew and passenger compartments was open, revealing the environment of instrument arrays and controls in which the pilots worked. A shoulder of each man, decorated with the ubiquitous Starflight symbol, was visible on each side of the central aisle, and Garamond could hear the preflight checks being carried out. Neither of the pilots looked back.

'Sit there,' Garamond whispered, pointing at a seat which was screened from the pilots' view by the main bulkhead. He put his fingers to his lips and winked at Chris, making it into a game. The boy nodded tautly, undeceived. Garamond went back to the entrance door and stood in it, waving to imaginary figures in the slidewalk tunnel, then went forward to the crew compartment.

'Take it away, Captain,' he said with the greatest joviality he could muster.

'Yes, sir.' The dark-chinned senior pilot glanced over his shoulder. 'As soon as Mrs Garamond and your son disembark.'

Garamond looked around the flight deck and found a small television screen showing a picture of the passenger compartment, complete with miniature images of Aileen and Chris. He wondered if the pilots had been watching it closely and how much they might have deduced from his actions.

'My wife and son are coming with us,' he said. 'Just for the ride.'

'I'm sorry, sir – their names aren't on my list.'

'This is a special arrangement I've just made with the President.'

'I'll have to check that with the tower.' There was a stubborn set to the pilot's bluish jaw as he reached for the communications switch.

'I assure you it's all right.' Garamond slid the pistol out of his jacket and used its barrel to indicate the runway ahead. 'Now, I want you to get all the normal clearances in a perfectly normal way and then do a maximum-energy ascent to my ship. I'm very familiar with the whole routine and I can fly this bug myself if necessary, so don't do any clever stuff which would make me shoot you.'

'I'm not going to get myself shot.' The senior pilot shrugged and his younger companion nodded vigorously. 'But how far do you think you're going to get, Captain?'

'Far enough – now take us out of here.' Garamond remained standing between the two seats. There was a subdued thud from the passenger door as it sealed itself, and then the shuttle surged forward. While monitoring the cross talk between the pilots and the North Field tower, Garamond studied the computer screen which was displaying flight parameters. The *Bissendorf* was in Polar Band One, the great stream of Starflight spacecraft – mainly population transfer vessels, but with a sprinkling of Exploratory Arm ships – which girdled the Earth at a height of more than a hundred kilometres. Incoming ships were allocated parking slots in any of the thirty-degree sectors marked by twelve space stations, their exact placing being determined by the amount of maintenance or repair they needed. The *Bissendorf* had been scheduled for a major refitting lasting three months, and was close in to Station 8, which the computer showed to be swinging up over the Aleutian Islands. A maximum-energy rendezvous could be accomplished in about eleven minutes.

'I take it you want to catch the *Bissendorf* this time round,' the senior pilot said as the shuttle's drive tubes built up thrust and the white runway markers began to flicker under its nose like tracer fire.

Garamond nodded. 'You take it right.'

'It's going to be rough on your wife and boy.' There was an unspoken question in the comment.

'Not as rough as . . .' Garamond decided to do the pilots a favour by telling them nothing – they too would be caught up in Elizabeth's enquiries.

'There's a metallizer aerosol in the locker beside you,' the co-pilot volunteered, speaking for the first time.

'Thanks.' Garamond found the aerosol container and passed it back to Aileen. 'Spray your clothes with this. Do Chris as well.'

'What's it for?' Aileen was trying to sound unconcerned, but her voice was small and cold.

'It won't do your clothes any harm, but it makes them react against the restraint field inside the ship when you move. It turns them into a kind of safety net and also stops you floating about when you're in free fall.' Garamond had forgotten how little Aileen knew about spaceflight or air travel. She had never even been in an ordinary jetliner, he recalled. The great age of air tourism was long past – if a person was lucky enough to live in an acceptable part of the Earth he tended to stay put.

'You can use it first,' Aileen said.

'I don't need it – all space fliers' uniforms are metallized

30

when they're made.' Garamond smiled encouragingly. *The pilot didn't know how right he was,* he thought. *This is going to be rough on my wife and boy.* He returned his attention to the pilots as the shuttle lifted its nose and cleared the ground. As soon as the undercarriage had been retracted and the craft was aerodynamically clean the drive tubes boosted it skywards on a pink flare of recombining ions. Garamond, standing behind the pilots, was pushed against the bulkhead and held there by the sustained acceleration. Behind him, Chris began to sob.

'Don't worry, son,' Garamond called. 'This won't last long. We'll soon be . . .'

'North Field to shuttlecraft Sahara Tango 4299,' a voice crackled from the radio. 'This is Fleet Commodore Keegan calling. Come in, please.'

'Don't answer that,' Garamond ordered. The clock behind his eyes had come to an abrupt and sickening halt.

'But that was Keegan himself. Are you mixed up in something big, Captain?'

'Big enough.' Garamond hesitated as the radio repeated its message. 'Tune that out and get me Commander Napier on my bridge.' He gave the pilot a microwave frequency which would by-pass the *Bissendorf*'s main communications room.

'But . . .'

'Immediately.' He raised the pistol against multiple gravities. 'This is a hair trigger and there's a lot of G-force piling up on my finger.'

'I'm making the call now.' The pilot spun a small vernier on the armrest of his chair and in a few seconds had established contact.

'Commander Napier here.' Garamond felt a surge of relief as he recognized the cautious tones Napier always employed when he did not know who was on the other end of a channel.

'This is an urgent one, Cliff.' Garamond spoke steadily. 'Have you had any communications about me from Starflight House?'

'Ah . . . no. Was I supposed to?'

'That doesn't matter now. Here's a special instruction which I'm asking you to obey immediately and without question. Do you understand?'

'Okay, Vance.' Napier sounded puzzled, but not suspicious or alarmed.

'I'm on the shuttle and will rendezvous with you in a few minutes, but right now I want you to throw the ultimate master switch on the external communications system. *Right now, Cliff !*'

There was a slight pause, during which Napier must have been considering the facts that what he had been asked to do was illegal and that under Starflight Regulations he was not obliged to obey such an order – then the channel went dead.

Garamond closed his eyes for a second. He knew that Napier had also thought about their years together on the *Bissendorf*, all the light-years they had covered, all the alien suns, all the hostile useless planets, all the disappointments which had studded their quest for *lebensraum*, all the bottles of whisky they had killed while in orbit around lost, lonely points of light both to console themselves and to make the next leg of a mission seem bearable. If he and Aileen and Chris had any chance of life it lay in the fact that a spaceship was an island universe, a tiny enclave in which Elizabeth's power was less than absolute. While in Earth orbit the ship's officers would have been forced to obey any direct order from Starflight Admincom, but he had successfully blocked the communications channels . . . A warning chime from the shuttle's computer interrupted Garamond's thoughts.

'We have some pretty severe course and speed corrections coming up,' the younger pilot said. 'Do you want to advise your wife ?'

Garamond nodded gratefully. The sky in the forward view panels had already turned from deep blue to black as the shuttle's tubes hurled it clear of the atmosphere. In a maximum-energy ballistic-style sortie it was understood that there was no time for niceties – the computer which was controlling the flight profile would subject passengers to as much stress, within pro-grammed limits, as they could stand. Garamond edged back-wards until he could see Aileen and Chris.

'Get ready for some rollercoaster stuff,' he told them. 'Don't try to fight the ship or you'll be sick. Just go with it and the restraint field will hold you in place.' They both nodded silently, in unison, eyes fixed on his face, and he felt a crushing sense of responsibility and guilt. He had barely finished speaking when a series of lateral corrections twisted space out of its normal shape, pulling him to the left and then upwards away from the floor. The fierce pressure of the bulkhead against his back prevented him from being thrown around but he guessed that his wife and son must have been lifted out of their seats. An involuntary gasp from Aileen confirmed her distress.

'It won't be long now,' he told her. Stars were shining in the blackness ahead of the shuttle, and superimposed on the random points of light was a strip of larger, brighter motes, most of which had visible irregularities of shape. Polar Band One glittered like a diamond bracelet, at the midpoint of which Sector Station 8 flared with a yellowish brilliance. The two distinct levels of luminosity, separating man-made objects from the background of distant suns, created a three-dimensional effect, an awareness of depth and cosmic scale which Garamond rarely experienced when far into a mission. He remained with the pilots, braced between their seats and the bulkhead, while the shuttle drew closer to the stream of orbiting spaceships and further corrections were applied to match speed and direction. By this time Starflight Admincom would have tried to contact the *Bissendorf* and would probably be taking other measures to prevent his escape.

'There's your ship,' the senior pilot commented, and the note of satisfaction in his voice put Garamond on his guard. 'It looks like you're a little late, Captain – there's another shuttle already drifting into its navel.'

Garamond, unused to orienting himself with the cluttered traffic of the Polar Band, had to search the sky for several seconds before he located the *Bissendorf* and was able to pick out the silvered bullet of a shuttle closing in on the big ship's transfer dock. He felt a cool prickling on his forehead. It was impossible for the other shuttle to have made better time on the haul up from Earth, but Admincom must have been able to divert one which was already in orbit and instruct it to block the *Bissendorf*'s single transfer dock.

'What do you want to do, Captain ?' The blue-chinned senior

pilot had begun to enjoy himself. 'Would you like to hand over that gun now?'

Garamond shook his head. 'The other shuttle's making a normal docking approach. Get in there before him.'

'It's too late.'

Garamond placed the muzzle of the pistol against the pilot's neck. 'Ram your nose into that dock, sonny.'

'You're crazy, but I'll try.' The pilot fixed his eyes on the expanding shape of the *Bissendorf*, then spun verniers to bring his sighting crosshairs on to the red-limned target of the dock which was already partially obscured by the other shuttle. As he did so the retro tubes began firing computer-controlled bursts which cut their forward speed. 'I told you it was too late.'

'Override the computer,' Garamond snapped. 'Kill those retros.'

'Do you want to commit suicide?'

'Do you?' Garamond pressed the pistol into the other man's spine and watched as he tripped out the autocontrol circuits. The image of the competing shuttle and the docking target expanded in the forward screen with frightening speed.

The pilot instinctively moved backwards in his seat. 'We're going to hit the other shuttle, for Christ's sake!'

'I know,' Garamond said calmly. 'And after we do you'll have about two seconds to get those crosshairs back on target. Now let's see how good you are.'

The other shuttle ballooned ahead of and slightly above them until they were looking right into its main driver tubes, there was a shuddering clang which Garamond felt in his bones, the shuttle vanished, and the vital docking target slewed away to one side. Events began to happen in slow motion for Garamond. He had time to monitor every move the pilot made as he fired emergency corrective jets which wrenched the ship's nose back on to something approximating its original bearing, time to brace himself as retros hammered on the craft's frame, even time to note and be grateful for the discovery that the pilot was good. Then the shuttle speared into the *Bissendorf*'s transfer dock at five times the maximum permitted speed and wedged itself into the interior arrester rings with a shrieking impact which deformed its hull.

Garamond, the only person on the shuttle not protected by a seat, was driven forward but was saved from injury by the restraint field's reaction against any violent movement of his clothing. He felt a surge of induced heat pass through the material, and at the same time became aware of a shrill whistling sound from the rear of the ship. A popping in his ears told him that air was escaping from the shuttle into the vacuum of the *Bissendorf*'s dock. A few seconds later Chris began to sob, quietly and steadily. Garamond went aft, knelt before the boy and tried to soothe him.

'What's happening, Vance?' The brightly-coloured silk of Aileen's dress was utterly incongruous.

'Rough docking, that's all. We're losing some air but they'll be pressurizing the dock and . . .' He hesitated as a warbling note came from the shuttle's address system. 'They've done it – that's the equalization signal to say we can get out now. There's nothing to worry about.'

'But we're falling.'

'We aren't falling, honey. Well, we are – but not downwards . . .' It came to Garamond that he had no time at that moment to introduce his wife to celestial mechanics. 'I want you and Chris to sit right here for a few minutes. Okay?'

He stood up, opened the passenger door and looked out at a group of officers and engineering personnel who had gathered on the docking bay's main platform. Among them was the burly figure of Cliff Napier. Garamond launched himself upwards from the sill and allowed the slight drag of the ship's restraint field to curve his weightless flight downwards on to the steel platform where his boots took a firm grip. Napier caught his arm while the other men were saluting.

'Are you all right, Vance? That was the hairiest docking I ever saw.'

'I'm fine. Explain it all later, Cliff. Get through to the engine deck and tell them I want immediate full power.'

'Immediate?'

'Yes – there's a streamer of nova dust lagging behind the main weather front and we're going to catch it. I presume you've preset the course.'

'But what about the shuttle and its crew?'

'We'll have to take the shuttle with us, Cliff. The shuttle and everybody on it.'

'I see.' Napier raised his wrist communicator to his lips and ordered full power. He was a powerfully built bull-necked man with hands like the scoops of a mechanical digger, but there was a brooding intelligence in his eyes. 'Is this our last mission for Starflight?'

'It's my last, anyway.' Garamond looked around to make sure nobody was within earshot. 'I'm in deep, Cliff – and I've dragged you in with me.'

'It was my decision – I didn't have to pull the plug on the communications boys. Are they coming after you?'

'With every ship that Starflight owns.'

'They won't catch us,' Napier said confidently as the deck began to press up under their feet, signalling that the *Bissendorf* was accelerating out of orbit. 'We'll ride that wisp of dust up the hill to Uranus, and when we've caught the tide . . . Well, there's a year's supplies on board.'

'Thanks.' Garamond shook hands with Napier, yet – while comforted by the blunt human contact – he wondered how long it would be before either of them would refer openly to the bitter underlying reality of their situation. They were all dressed up with a superb ship. But a century of exploration by the vast Starflight armada had proved one thing.

There was nowhere to go.

four

They were able to put off the decision for three days.

During that time there was only one direction in which the *Bissendorf* could logically go – towards the galactic south, in pursuit of the single vagrant wisp of particles which lingered behind the retreating weather fronts. They had caught it, barely, and the vast insubstantial ramjets formed by the ship's magnetic fields had begun to gather power, boosting it towards light-speed and beyond. It was the prototypes of starships such as the *Bissendorf* which, a century earlier, had all but demolished Einsteinian physics. On the first tentative flights there had been something of the predicted increase in mass, but no time dilation effect, no impenetrable barrier at the speed of light. A new physics had been devised – based mainly on the work of the Canadian mathematician, Arthur Arthur – which took into account the lately observed fact that when a body of appreciable mass and gravitic field reached speeds approaching .2C it entered new frames of reference. Once a ship crossed the threshold velocity it created its own portable universe in which different rules applied, and it appeared that the great universal constant was not the speed of light. It was time itself.

On his earlier missions Garamond had been grateful that Einstein's work had its limitations and that time did not slow down for the space traveller – he would have had no stomach for finding his wife ageing ten years for his one, or having a son who quickly grew older than himself. But on this voyage, his last for Starflight, with Aileen and Christopher aboard, it would have resolved many difficulties had he been able to trace a vast circle across one part of the galaxy and return to Earth to find, as promised by Einstein, that Elizabeth Lindstrom was long dead. Arthurian physics had blocked that notional escape door, however, and he was faced with the question of where to go in his year of stolen time.

His thinking on the matter was influenced by two major considerations. The first was that he had no intention of condemning the 450-strong crew of the *Bissendorf* to a slow death in an unknown part of the galaxy in a year's time. The ship had to return to Earth and therefore his radius of action was limited to the distance it could cover in six months. Even supposing he travelled in a straight line to one preselected destination, the six-month limitation meant he would not reach far beyond the volume of space already totally explored by Starflight. Chances of this one desperate flight producing a habitable world on which to hide had been microscopic to begin with; when modified by the distance factor they vanished into realms of fantasy.

The other major consideration was a personal one. Garamond already knew where he wanted to go, but was having trouble justifying the decision.

*

'Cluster 803 is your best bet,' Clifford Napier said. He was leaning back in a simulated leather chair in Garamond's quarters, and in his hand was a glass of liqueur whisky which he had not yet tasted but was holding up to the light to appreciate its colour. His heavy-lidded brown eyes were inscrutable as he continued with his thesis.

'You can make it with time to spare. It's dense – average distance between suns half a light-year – so you'd be able to check a minimum of eight systems before having to pull out. And it's prime exploration territory, Vance. As you know, the S.E.A. Board recommended that 803 should be given high priority when the next wave is being planned.'

Garamond sipped his own whisky, with its warmth of forgotten summers. 'It makes sense, all right.' The two men sat without speaking for a time, listening to the faint hum of the ship's superconducting flux pumps which was always present even in the engineered solitude of the skipper's rooms.

'It makes sense,' Napier said finally, 'but you don't want to go there. Right?'

'Well, maybe it makes too much sense. Admincom could predict that we'd head for 803 and send a hundred ships into the region. A thousand ships.'

'Think they could catch us?'

'There's always that chance,' Garamond said. 'It's been proved that four flickerwings getting just ahead of another and matching velocities can control it better than its own skipper just by deciding how much reaction mass to let slip by.'

There was another silence, then Napier gave a heavy sigh. 'All right, Vance – where's your map?'

'Which map?'

'The one showing Pengelly's Star. That's where you want to go, isn't it?'

Garamond felt a surge of anger at having his innermost thoughts divined so accurately by the other man. 'My father actually met Rufus Pengelly once,' he said defensively. 'He told me he'd never known a man less capable of trickery – and if there was one thing my father could do it was judge character just by . . .' He broke off as Napier began to laugh.

'Vance, you don't need to sell the idea to me. We're not going to find the third world, so it doesn't matter where we go, does it?'

Garamond's anger was replaced by a growing sense of relief. He went to his desk, opened a drawer and took out four large photoprints which appeared to be of greyish metallic or stone surfaces on which were arranged a number of darker spots in a manner suggestive of star maps. The fuzziness of the markings and the blotchy texture of the background were due to the fact that the prints were computer reconstructions of star charts which had been destroyed by fire.

A special kind of fire, Garamond thought. *The one which robbed us of a neighbour.*

Sagania had been discovered early in the exploratory phase. It was less than a hundred light-years from Sol, only a quarter of the separation the best statisticians had computed as the average for technical civilizations throughout the galaxy. Even more remarkable was the coincidence of timescales. In the geological lifespans of Sagania and Earth the period in which intelligent life developed and flourished represented less than a second in the life of a man, yet the fantastic gamble had come off. Saganians and Men had coexisted, against all the odds, within interstellar hailing distance, each able to look into the night sky and see the other's parent sun without optical aid. Both had taken the machine-using philosophy as far as the tapping of nuclear energy. Both had shared the outward urge, planned the building of starships, and – with their sub-beacons trembling in the blackness like candles in far-off windows – it was inevitable that there would have been a union.

Except that one day on Sagania – at a time when the first civilizations were being formed in the Valley of the Two Rivers on Earth – somebody had made a mistake. It may have been a politician who overplayed his hand, or a scientist who dealt the wrong cards, but the result was that Sagania lost its atmosphere, and its life, in an uncontrolled nuclear reaction which surged around the planet like a tidal wave of white fire.

Archaeologists from Earth, arriving seven thousand years later, had been able to discover very little about the final phase of Saganian civilization. Ironically or justly, according to one's point of view, the beings who had represented the peak of the planet's culture were the ones who removed virtually all trace of their existence. It was the older, humbler Saganian culture which, protected by the crust of centuries, had been uncovered by the electronic probes. Among the artifacts turned up were fragments of star maps which excited little comment, even though a few researchers had noticed that some of them showed a star which did not exist.

'This is the earliest fragment,' Garamond said, setting the photoprint on a table beside Napier. He pointed at a blurry speck. 'And that's the sun we've christened Pengelly's Star. Here's another map tentatively dated five hundred years later, and as you see – no Pengelly's Star. One explanation is that at some time between when these two maps were drawn the star vanished.'

'Maybe it got left out by mistake,' Napier prompted, aware that Garamond wanted to go over all the familiar arguments once more.

'That can't be – because we have two later maps, covering the same region but drawn several centuries apart, and they don't record the star either. And a visual check right now shows nothing in that region.'

'Which proves it died.'

'That's the obvious explanation. A quick but unspectacular flare-up – then extinction. Now here's the fourth map, the one found by Doctor Pengelly. As you can see, this map shows our star.'

'Which proves it's older than maps two and three.'

'Pengelly claims he excavated it at the highest level of all, that it's the youngest.'

'Which proves he was a liar. This sort of thing has happened before, Vance.' Napier flicked the glossy prints with blunt fingers. 'What about that affair in Crete a few hundred years ago? Archaeologists are always . . .'

'Trying to win acclaim for themselves. Pengelly had nothing to gain by lying about where he found the fragment. I personally believe it was drawn only a matter of decades before the Big Burn, well into the Saganians space-going era.' Garamond spoke with the flatness of utter conviction. 'You'll notice that on the fourth map the star isn't represented by a simple dot. There are traces of a circle around it.'

Napier shrugged and took the first sip of his whisky. 'It was a map showing the positions of extinct suns.'

'That's a possibility. Possibly even a probability, but I'm betting that Saganian space technology was more advanced than we suspect. I'm betting that Pengelly's Star was important to them in some way we don't understand. They might have found a habitable world there.'

'It wouldn't be habitable now. Not after its sun dying.'

'No – but there might be other maps, underground installations, anything.' Garamond suddenly heard his own words as though they were being spoken by a stranger, and he was appalled at the flimsiness of the logical structure which supported his family's hopes for a future. He glanced instinctively at the door leading to the bedroom where Aileen and Chris were asleep. Napier, perceptive as ever, did not reply and for a while they drank in silence. Blocks of coloured light, created for

41

decorative purposes by the same process which produced solid-image weather maps, drifted through the air of the room in random patterns, mingling and merging. Their changing reflections seemed to animate the gold snail on Garamond's desk.

'We never found any Saganian starships,' Napier said.

'It doesn't mean they didn't have them. You'd find their ships anywhere *but* in the vicinity of a burnt-out home world.' There was another silence and the light-cubes continued to drift through the room like prisms of insubstantial gelatin.

Napier finished his drink and got up to refill his glass. 'You're almost making some kind of a case, but why did the Exploratory Arm never follow it up?'

'Let's level with each other,' Garamond said. 'How many years is it since you really believed that Starflight wants to find other worlds?'

'I . . .'

'They've got Terranova, which they sell off in hectare lots as if it was a Long Island development property in the old days. They've got all the ships, too. Man's destiny is in the stars – just so long as he is prepared to sign half his life away to Starflight for the ride, and the other half for a plot of land. It's a smooth-running system, Cliff, and a few cheap new worlds showing up would spoil it. That's why there are so few ships, comparatively speaking, in the S.E.A.'

'But . . .'

'They're more subtle than the railroad and mining companies in the States were when they set up their private towns, but the technique's the same. What are you trying to say?'

'I'm trying to agree with you.' Napier punched his fist through a cube of lime-green radiance which floated away unaffected. 'It doesn't matter a damn where we go in this year, so let's hunt down Pengelly's Star. Have you any idea where it ought to be?'

'Some. Have a look at this chart.' As they walked over to the universal machine in the corner Garamond felt a sense of relief that Napier had been so easy to convince – to his own mind it gave the project a semblance of sanity. When he was within voice-acceptance range of the machine he called up the map it had prepared for him. A three-dimensional star chart appeared in the air above the console. One star trailed a curving wake of glowing red dashes in contrast to the solid green lines which represented the galactic drift of the others.

'I had no direct data on how far Pengelly's Star was from Sagania,' Garamond said. 'But the fact that we're interested in it carries the implication that it was a Sol-type sun. This gives an approximate value for its intrinsic luminosity and, as the dot representing it on the earliest Saganian map was about equal in size to other existing stars of first magnitude, I was able to assign a distance from Sagania.'

'There's a lot of assuming and assigning going on there,' Napier said doubtfully.

'Not all that much. Now, the stars throughout the entire region share the same proper motion and speed so, although they've all travelled a long way in seven thousand years, we can locate Pengelly's Star on this line with a fair degree of certainty.'

'Certainty, he says. What's the computed journey time? About four months?'

'Less if there's the right sort of dust blowing around.'

'It'll be there,' Napier said in a neutral voice. 'It's an ill wind . . .'

Later, when Napier had left to get some sleep, Garamond ordered the universal machine to convert an entire wall of the room into a forward-looking viewscreen. He sat for a long time in a deep chair, his drink untouched, staring at the stars and thinking about Napier's final remark. Part of the invisible galactic winds from which the *Bissendorf* drew its reaction mass had been very ill winds for somebody, sometime, somewhere. Heavy particles, driven across the galactic wheel by the forces of ancient novae, were the richest and most sought-after harvest of all. An experienced flickerwing man could tell when his engine intakes had begun to feed on such a cloud just by feeling the deck grow more insistent against his feet. But a sun going nova engulfed its planets, converting them and everything on them to incandescent gas, and at each barely perceptible surge of the ship Garamond wondered if his engines were feeding on the ghosts of dawn-time civilizations, obliterating all their dreams, giving the final answer to all their questions.

He fell asleep sitting at the viewscreen, on the dark edge of the abyss.

*

Aileen Garamond had been ill for almost a week.

Part of the trouble was due to shock and the subsequent stress of being catapulted into a difficult environment, but Garamond was surprised to discover that his wife was far more sensitive than he to minute changes in acceleration caused by the ship crossing weather zones. He explained to her that the *Bissendorf* relied largely on interstellar hydrogen for reaction mass, ionizing it by continuously firing electron beams ahead of the ship, then sweeping it up with electromagnetic fields which guided it through the engine intakes. As the distribution of hydrogen was constant the ship would have had constant acceleration, and its crew would have enjoyed an unchanging apparent gravity, had there been no other considerations. Space, however, was not the quiescent vacuum described by the old Earth-bound astronomers. Vagrant clouds of charged particles from a dozen different kinds of sources swept through it like winds and tides, heavy and energetic, clashing, deflecting, creating silent storms where they met each other head-on.

'On available hydrogen alone our best acceleration would be half a gravity or less,' Garamond said. 'That's why we value the high-activity regions and, where possible, plot courses which take us through them. And that's why you feel occasional changes in your weight.'

Aileen thought for a moment. 'Couldn't you vary the efficiency of the engines to compensate for those changes ?'

'Hey!' Garamond gave a pleased laugh. 'That's the normal practice on a passenger ship. They run at roughly nine tenths of full power and this is automatically stepped up or down as the ship enters poor or rich volumes of space, so that shipboard gravity remains constant. But Exploratory Arm ships normally keep going full blast, and on a trip like this one . . .' Garamond fell silent.

'Go on, Vance.' Aileen sat up in the bed, revealing her familiar tawny torso. 'You can't take it easy when you're being hunted.'

'It isn't so much that we're being hunted, it's just that to make the best use of our time we ought to move as fast as possible.'

Aileen got out of the bed and came towards where he was seated, her nakedness incongruous in the functional surroundings of his quarters. 'There's no point in our going to Terranova, is there? Isn't that what you're telling me?'

He leaned his face against the warm cushion of her belly. 'The ship can keep going for about a year. After that . . .'

'And we won't find a new planet. One we can live on, I mean.'

'There's always the chance.'

'How much of a chance?'

'It has taken the entire fleet a hundred years of searching to find one habitable planet. Work it out for yourself.'

'I see.' Aileen stood with him for a moment, almost abstractedly holding his face against herself, then she turned away with an air of purpose. 'It's about time for that guided tour of the ship you promised Christopher and me.'

'Are you sure you're feeling well enough?'

'I'll get well enough,' she assured him.

Garamond suddenly felt happier than he had expected to be ever again. He nodded and went into the main room where Chris was eating breakfast. As soon as the boy had got over his unfortunate introduction to spaceflight on board the shuttle, he had adapted quickly and easily to his new surroundings. Garamond had eased things as much as possible by putting in very little time in the *Bissendorf*'s control room, allowing Napier and the other senior officers to run the ship. He helped his son to dress and by the time he had finished Aileen had joined them, looking slightly self-conscious in the dove-grey nurse's coverall he had ordered for her from the quartermaster.

'You look fine,' he said before she could ask the age-old question.

Aileen examined herself critically. 'What was wrong with my dress?'

45

'Nothing, if you're on the recreation deck, but you must wear functional clothing when moving about the other sections of the ship. There aren't any other wives on board, and I don't like to rub it in.'

'But you told me a third of the crew were women.'

'That's right. We have a hundred-and-fifty female crew of varying ages and rank. On a long trip there's always a lot of short-term coupling going on, and occasionally there's a marriage, but no woman is taken on for purely biological reasons. Everybody has a job to do.'

'Don't sound so stuffy, Vance.' Aileen looked down at Christopher, then back at her husband. 'What about Christopher? Does everybody know why we're here?'

'No. I blocked the communications channels while we were on the shuttle. The one other person on board who knows the whole story is Cliff Napier – all the others can only guess I'm in some sort of a jam, but they won't be too concerned about it.' Garamond smiled as he remembered the old flickerwingers' joke. 'It's a kind of relativity effect – the faster and farther you go, the smaller the President gets.'

'Couldn't they have heard about it on the radio since then?'

Garamond shook his head emphatically. 'It's impossible to communicate with a ship when it's under way. No signal can get through the fields. The crew will probably decide I walked out on Elizabeth the way a commander called Witsch once did. If anything, I'll go up in their estimation.'

It took more than an hour to tour the various sections and levels of the *Bissendorf*, starting with the command deck and moving 'downwards' through the various administrative, technical and workshop levels to the field generating stations, and the pods containing the flux pumps and hydrogen fusion plant. At the end of the tour Garamond realized, with a dull sense of astonishment, that for a while he had managed to forget that he and his family were under sentence of death.

*

Boosted by the ion-rich tides of space, the ship maintained an average acceleration of 13 metres per second squared. Punishing though this was to the crew, whose weight had apparently increased by one third, it was a rate of speed-increase which would have required several months before the Bissendorf *could have reached the speed of light under Einsteinian laws. After only seven weeks, however, the ship had attained a speed of fifty million metres a second – the magical threshold figure above which Arthurian physics held sway – and new phenomena, inexplicable in terms of low-speed systems, were observed. To those on board acceleration remained constant, yet the* Bissendorf's *speed increased sharply until, at the mid-point of the voyage, only twelve days later, it was travelling at vast multiples of the speed of light.*

Retardation produced a mirror image of the distance-against-time graph, and in an elapsed time of four months the ship was in the computed vicinity of Pengelly's Star.

*

'I'm sorry, Vance.' Cliff Napier's heavy-boned face was sombre as he spoke. 'There's just no sign of it. Yamoto says that if we were within ten light-years of a black sun his instruments couldn't miss it.'

'Is he positive?'

'He's positive. In fact, according to him there's less spatial background activity than normal.'

I'm not going to let it happen, Garamond thought irrationally. Aloud he said, 'Let's go down to the observatory – I want to talk to Yamoto about this.'

'I'll put him on your viewer now.'

'No, I want to see him in person.' Garamond left the central command console and nodded to Gunther, the second exec, to take over. This was the moment he had been dreading since the *Bissendorf's* engines had been shut down an hour earlier, making it possible – in the absence of the all-devouring intake fields – to carry out radiation checks of the surrounding space. The reason he was going to the observatory in person was that he had a sudden need to move his arms and legs, to respond to the crushing sense of urgency which had been absent while the ship was in flight and now was back with him again. He wanted some time away from the watchful eyes of the bridge personnel.

'I'm sorry, Vance.' Napier always had trouble adjusting to zero-gravity conditions and his massive figure swayed precariously as he walked in magnetic boots to the elevator shaft.

'You said that before.'

'I know, but I'd begun to believe we were on to something, and somehow I feel guilty over the way it has turned out.'

'That's crazy—we always knew it was a long shot,' Garamond said. *You liar,* he told himself. *You didn't believe it was a long shot at all. You had convinced yourself you'd find a signpost to the third world because you couldn't face the fact that you condemned your wife and son to death.*

As the elevator was taking him down he thought back, for perhaps the thousandth time, to that afternoon on the terrace at Starflight House. All he had had to do was keep an eye on Harald Lindstrom, to refuse when asked for permission to run, to do what anybody else would have done in the same circumstances. Instead, he had let the boy trick him into doing his hardened spacefarer bit, then he had allowed himself to be pressured, then he had turned his back and indulged in daydreams while Harald was climbing, then he had been too slow in reaching the statue while the first fatal millimetre of daylight opened up between the boy's fingers and the metal construction and he was falling . . . and falling . . . *falling.*

'Here we are.' Napier opened the elevator door, revealing a tunnel-like corridor at the end of which was the *Bissendorf*'s astronomical observatory.

'Thanks.' Garamond fought to suppress a sense of unreality as he walked out of the elevator. He saw, as in a dream, the white-clad figure of Sammy Yamoto standing at the far end of the corridor waving to him. His brain was trying in a numbed way to deal with the paradox that moments of truth, those instants when reality cannot be avoided, always seem unreal. And the truth was that his wife and child were going to die. *Because of him.*

'For a man who found nothing,' Napier commented, 'Sammy Yamoto's looking pretty excited.'

Garamond summoned his mind back from grey wanderings.

Yamoto came to meet him, plum-coloured lips trembling slightly. 'We've found something! After I spoke to Mister Napier I became curious over the fact that there was less matter per cubic centimetre than the galactic norm. It was as if the region had been swept by a passing sun, yet there was no sun around.'

'What did you find?'

'I'd already checked out the electro-magnetic spectrum and knew there couldn't *be* a sun nearby, but I got a crazy impulse and checked the gravitic spectrum anyway.' Yamoto was a fifty-year-old man who had looked on many worlds in his lifetime, yet his face was the face of a man in shock. Garamond felt the first stirrings of a powerful elation.

'Go on,' Napier said from behind him.

'I found a gravity source of stellar magnitude less than a tenth of a light-year away, so . . .'

'I knew it!' Napier's voice was hoarse. 'We've found Pengelly's Star.'

Garamond's eyes were locked on the astronomer's. 'Let Mister Yamoto speak.'

'So I took some tachyonic readings to get an approximation of the object's size and surface composition, and . . . You aren't going to believe this, Mister Garamond.'

'Try me,' Garamond said.

'As far as I can tell . . .' Yamoto swallowed painfully. 'As far as I can tell, the object out there . . . the thing we have discovered is a spaceship over three hundred million kilometres in diameter!'

five

Like everyone else on board the *Bissendorf*, Garamond spent a lot of time at the forward viewscreens during the long days of the approach to the sphere.

He attended many meetings, accompanied by Yamoto who had become one of the busiest and most sought-after men on the ship. At first the Chief Astronomer had wanted to take advantage of the drive shut-down period to get a tachyonic signal announcing his discovery off to Earth. Garamond discreetly did not point out his own role as prime mover in the find. Instead he made Yamoto aware of the danger of letting fame-hungry professional rivals appear on the scene too early, and at the same time he insured against risks by ordering an immediate engine restart.

Yamoto went back to work, but the curious thing was that even after a full week of concentrated activity he knew little more about the sphere than had been gleaned in his first hurried scan. He confirmed that it had a diameter of some 320,000,000 kilometres, or just over two astronomical units; he confirmed that its surface was smooth to beyond the limits of resolution, certainly the equivalent of finely machined steel; he confirmed that the sphere emitted no radiation other than on the gravitic spectrum, and that analysis of this proved it to be hollow. In that week the only new data he produced were that the object's sphericity was perfect to within the possible margin of error, and that it rotated. On the question of whether it was a natural or an artificial object he would venture no professional opinion.

Garamond turned all these factors over in his mind, trying to gauge their relevance to his own situation. The sphere, whatever its nature, no matter what its origins might be, was a startling find – the fact that it had been indicated on an antique Saganian star chart radically altered the accepted views about the dead race's technological prowess. Possibly the whole science of astronomy would be affected, but not the pathetically short futures of his wife and child. What had he been hoping for? A fading sun which still emitted some life-giving warmth? An Earth-type planet with a vast network of underground caverns leading down into the heat of its core? A race of friendly humanoids who would say, 'Come and live with us and we'll protect your family from the President of Starflight'?

It was in the nature of hope that it could survive on such preposterous fantasies. But only when they were confined to the subconscious, where – as long as they existed at all – the emotions could equate them with genuine prospects of survival, enabling the man on the scaffold steps to retain his belief that something could still turn up to save him. Garamond and his wife and boy were on the scaffold steps, and the fantasies of hope were being dissipated by the awful presence of the sphere.

Garamond found that trying to comprehend its size produced an almost physical pain between his temples. The object was big enough by astronomical standards, so large that with Sol positioned at its centre the Earth's orbit would be within the shell, assuming that the outer surface was a shell. It was so huge that, from distances which would have reduced Sol to nothing more than a bright star, it was clearly visible to the unaided eye as a disc of blackness against the star clouds of the galactic lens. Garamond watched it grow and grow in his screens until it filled the entire field of view with its dark, inconceivable bulk – and yet it was still more than 150,000,000 kilometres away.

Something within him began to cringe from it. In the early stages of the approach he had nursed the idea that, because of the smoothness of its surface, the sphere had to be an artifact. The notion faded when exposed to the mind-punishing reality of the sphere's magnitude, because there was no way to visualize engineering on that scale, to conceive of a technology so far beyond anything mankind could dream of achieving. Then, in the final stages of the approach, the *Bissendorf*'s sensors became aware of a planet orbiting outside the sphere.

There was no optical evidence of the planet's existence, but a study of its gravitic emissions showed that it was of approximately the same diameter and mass as Earth, and that its almost-circular orbit lay some 80,000,000 kilometres outside the sphere's surface. Although the discovery of the planet was of value in itself, the real importance lay in what could now be deduced about the nature of the sphere.

Chief Astronomer Yamoto sent Garamond a report which stated, unequivocally, that it was a thin shell enclosing an otherwise normal sun.

*

By the time the ship had matched velocities with the hidden star and slipped into an equatorial parking orbit, it was just over two thousand kilometres from the surface of the dark sphere. The range was inconvenient for the rocket-propelled buggy which would carry the exploration party, but the *Bissendorf* had never been intended for close manoeuvring, and Garamond decided against jockeying in closer with the rarely-used ion tubes. He sat in the central control area and watched the stereo image of the EVA group as they prepared themselves in the muster station. Garamond knew all the men and women of his crew by sight if not by name, but there was one blond fresh-complexioned youngster he was having trouble identifying. He pointed at the screen.

'Cliff, is that one of the shuttle crew we shanghaied?'

'That's right. Joe Braunek. He fitted in well,' Napier said. 'I think you did him a favour.'

'Did Tayman select him for this mission?'

'He volunteered. Tayman referred it back to me and I interviewed Braunek in person.' Napier broke off to contemplate a memory which appeared to amuse him.

'Well?'

'He says he's entitled to log the flying time because you wrecked his shuttle and dumped it near Saturn.'

Garamond nodded his approval. 'What about the other shuttle pilot? The one with the blue chin.'

'Shrapnel? Ah . . . he didn't fit in so well. In fact, he's pretty resentful. He wouldn't sign on the crew and I've had to keep him under surveillance.'

'Oh? I seem to remember sending him an apology.'

'You did. He's still resentful.'

'I wonder why?'

Napier gave a dry cough. 'He wasn't planning to be separated from his wife for this length of time.'

'I'm a self-centred bastard – is that it, Cliff?'

'Nothing like it.'

'Don't give me that – I recognize that Chopin cough you get every time I go off the rails.' Garamond visualized the shuttle pilot, tried to imagine the man in the context of a family like his own, but found the exercise strangely difficult. 'Shrapnel knows he'll only be away for a year. Why doesn't he try to make the best of it?'

Napier coughed once more. 'The EVA group are about ready to go.'

'Your TB is back again, Cliff. What did I say that time?' Garamond stared hard at his next-in-command.

Napier took a deep breath, altering the slopes of his massive chest and shoulders. 'You don't like Shrapnel, and he doesn't like you, and that amuses me – because you're both the same type. If you were in his shoes *you'd* be broody and resentful and looking for an opportunity to twist things back the way you wanted them. He even looks a bit like you, yet you sit there telling everybody he's weird.'

Garamond gave a smile he did not feel. Napier and he had long ago discarded all remnants of formal relationship, and he felt no resentment at the other man's words, but he found them disturbing. They had implications he did not want to examine. He selected the EVA group's intercom frequency and listened to the clamorous, overlapping voices of the men as the buggy was sealed and the dock evacuation procedure began. They were complaining in a good-natured way about the discomfort of the space-suits which they normally donned only twice a year in practice drills, or about the difficulty of carrying instruments and tool kits in gloved hands, but Garamond knew they were genuinely excited. Life on board an S.E.A. vessel consisted of routine outward journeys, brief pauses while it was established by long range instruments that the target suns had no planets or no usable planets, and equally dull returns to base. This was the first occasion in the *Bissendorf*'s entire span of service on which it had been necessary for men to leave its protective hull and venture into alien space with the object of making physical contact with something outside humanity's previous experience. It was a big moment for the little exploratory team and Garamond found himself wishing he could take part.

He watched as the outer doors of the dock slid aside to reveal a blackness which was unrelieved by stars. At a distance of two thousand kilometres the sphere not only filled one half of the sky, it *was* one half of the sky. The observed universe was cut into two hemispheres – one of them glowing with starclouds, the other filled with light-absorbent darkness. There was no sensation of being close to a huge object, rather one of being poised above infinite deeps.

The restraining rings opened and allowed the white-painted buggy to jet out clear of the mother ship. Its boxy, angular outline shrank to invisibility in a few seconds, but its interior and marker lights remained in view for quite a long time as the craft moved 'downwards' from the *Bissendorf*. Garamond stayed at central control while the buggy descended, watching several screens at once as its cameras sent back different types of information. At a height of three hundred metres the buggy's commander, Kraemer, switched on powerful searchlights and succeeded in creating a greyish patch of illumination on the sphere's surface.

'Instruments show zero gravity at surface,' he reported.

Garamond cut in on the circuit. 'Do you want to go on down?'

'Yes, sir. The surface looks metallic from here – I'd like to try a touchdown with magnetic clamps.'

'Go ahead.'

The indistinct greyness expanded on the screens until the clang of the buggy's landing gear was heard. 'It's no use,' Kraemer said. 'We just bounced off.'

'Are you going to let her float?'

'No, sir. I'm going to go in again and maintain some drive

pressure. That should lock the buggy in place against the surface and give us a fixed point to work from.'

'Go ahead, Kraemer.' Garamond looked at Napier and nodded in satisfaction. The two men watched as the buggy was inched into contact with the surface and held there by the thrust of its tubes.

Kraemer's voice was heard again. 'Surface seems to have a reasonable index of friction – we aren't slipping around. I think it's safe to go out for samples.'

'Proceed.'

The buggy's door slid open, spacesuited figures drifted out and formed a small swarm around the splayed-out landing gear. Bracing themselves against the tubular legs, the figures went to work on the vaguely seen surface of the sphere with drills, cutters and chemicals. At the end of thirty minutes, by which time the team operating the valency cutter could have sliced through a house-sized block of chrome steel, nobody had managed even to mark the surface. The result was in accordance with Garamond's premonitions.

'This is a new one on me,' said Harmer, the chemist. 'We can't make a spectroscopic analysis because the stuff refuses to burn. At this stage I can't even say for sure that it's a metal. We're just wasting our time down here.'

'Tell Kraemer to bring them up,' Garamond said to Napier. 'Is there any point in firing the main ionizing gun against it ?'

'None at all,' put in Denise Serra, the Chief Physicist. 'If a valency cutter at a range of one centimetre achieved nothing there's no point in hosing energy all over it from this distance.'

Garamond nodded. 'Okay. Let's pool our ideas. We've acquired a little more information, although most of it is negative, and I'd like to have your thoughts on whether the sphere is a natural object or an artifact.'

'It's an artifact,' Denise Serra said immediately, with characteristic firmness. 'Its sphericity is perfect and the surface is smooth to limits of below one micron. Nature doesn't operate that way – at least, not on the astronomical scale.' She glanced a challenge at Yamoto.

55

'I have to agree,' Yamoto said. 'I've been avoiding the idea, but I can't conceive of any natural mechanism which would produce that thing out there. However, that doesn't mean I can see how it was constructed by intelligent beings. It's just too much.' He shook his head dispiritedly. The haggardness of his face showed that he had been losing a lot of sleep.

O'Hagan, the Chief Science Officer, who was a stickler for protocol, cleared his throat and spoke for the first time. 'Our difficulties arise from the fact that the *Bissendorf* is an exploration vessel and very little more. The correct procedure now would be to send a tachyon signal back to Earth and get a properly equipped expedition out here.' His severe grey gaze held steadily on Garamond's face.

'That's outside the scope of the present discussion,' Napier said.

Garamond shook his head. 'No, it isn't. Gentlemen, and lady, Mister O'Hagan has put into words something which must have been on all your minds since the beginning of this mission. It can't have been difficult for you to work out for yourselves that I'm in trouble with Starflight House. In fact, it's personal trouble with Elizabeth Lindstrom – and I think you all know what that means. I'm not going to give you any more details, simply because I don't want you to be involved any more than you are at present.

'Perhaps it is enough to say that this has to be my last voyage as a Starflight commander, and I want this year in full.'

O'Hagan looked pained, but he held his ground doggedly. 'I'm sure I'm speaking for all the other section heads when I say that we feel the utmost personal loyalty to Captain Garamond, and that our feelings aren't affected by the circumstances surrounding the start of this voyage. Had it turned out to be a normal, uneventful mission I, for one, wouldn't have considered questioning its legality – but the fact remains that we have made the most important discovery since Terranova and Sagania, and I feel it should be reported to Earth without delay.'

'I disagree,' Napier said coldly. 'Starflight House didn't direct the *Bissendorf* to this point in space. The sphere was discovered

56

because Captain Garamond acted independently to check out a personally-held theory. We'll hand it over to Starflight, as a bonus they didn't earn, at the end of the mission's scheduled span of one year.'

O'Hagan gave a humourless smile. 'I still feel . . .'

Napier jumped to his feet. 'What do you mean when you say you *feel*, Mister O'Hagan ? Don't you think with your brain like the rest of us ? Does the fact that you *feel* these things turn them into something for which you have no personal responsibility ?'

'That's enough,' Garamond said.

'I just want O'Hagan to stand over his words.'

'I said . . .'

'Gentlemen, I withdraw my remarks,' O'Hagan interrupted, staring fixedly at his notepad. 'It wasn't my intention to divert the discussion away from the main topic. Now, we seem agreed that the sphere is of artificial origin – so what is its purpose ?' He raised his eyes and scanned the assembled officers.

There was a lengthy silence.

'Defence ?' Denise Serra's round face mirrored her doubts. 'Is there a planet inside ?'

'There might be a planet on the far side of the sun which hasn't shown up much on our gravitic readings.' Yamoto said. 'But if we had the technology to produce that sphere, could there be an enemy so powerful that we would have to cower behind a shield ?'

'Supposing it was a case of "Stop the galaxy, I want to get off" ? Maybe the builders were pacifists and felt the need to hide. They made a pretty good job of concealing a star.'

'I hope that isn't the answer,' Yamoto said gloomily. 'If *they* needed to hide . . .'

'This is getting too speculative,' Garamond put in. 'The immediate practical question is, does it have an entrance ? Can we get inside ? Let's have your thoughts on that.'

Yamoto stroked his wispy beard. 'If there is an entrance, it ought to be on the equator so that ships could hold their positions over it just by going into a parking orbit the way we did.'

'So you suggest doing a circuit of the sphere in the equatorial plane ?'

'Yes – in the opposite direction to its rotation. That way we would get the advantage of its seventy thousand kilometres an hour equatorial rotation and cut down on our own G-forces.'

'That's decided then,' Garamond said. 'We'll turn around as soon as Kraemer and his team are on board. I hope we'll recognize an entrance if we find one.'

*

Three duty periods later he was asleep beside Aileen when his personal communicator buzzed him into wakefulness.

'Garamond here,' he said quietly, trying not to disturb his wife.

'Sorry to disturb you, Vance,' Napier said, 'but I think we're going to reach an entrance to the sphere in a couple of hours from now.'

'*What?*' Garamond sat upright, aware of deceleration forces. 'How could you tell?'

'Well, we can't be certain, but it's the most likely explanation for the echoes we're picking up on the long-range radar.'

'What sort of echoes?'

'A lot of them, Vance. There's a fleet of about three thousand ships in parking orbit, dead ahead of us.'

six

The ships were invisible to the naked eye, yet on the detector screens on board the *Bissendorf* they appeared as a glowing swarm, numerous as stars in a dense cluster. High-resolution radar, aided by other forms of sensory apparatus, revealed them to be of many different sizes and shapes, a vast and variegated armada poised above one point on the enigmatic sphere.

'You could have told me they weren't Starflight ships,' Garamond said, easing himself into his seat in central control, his eyes fixed on the forward screens.

'Sorry, Vance – it didn't occur to me.' Napier handed Garamond a bulb of hot coffee. 'As soon as I saw the lack of standard formations I knew they couldn't be Starflight vessels. The silhouettes and estimated masses produced by the computers confirmed it – none of the ships in that bunch can be identified by type.'

Second Officer Gunther gave a quiet laugh. 'That was a pretty nervy moment up here.'

Garamond smiled in sympathy. 'I guess it was.'

'Then we realized we were looking at a collection of hulks.'

'You're positive?'

'There's no radiation of any kind. Those are dead ships, and they've been that way for a long time.' Napier shook his head. 'This is turning out to be one hell of a trip, Vance. First there was the sphere itself, and now . . . We always wondered why no Saganian starships had ever been found.'

One hell of a trip, Garamond repeated to himself, his mind trying to deal with the magnitude of the new discovery and at the same time cope with the shocking and unexpected presence of something akin to hope. He had fled from the Earth as an obscure flickerwing commander, but now had the prospect of returning as the most celebrated explorer since Laker had founded Terranova and Molyneaux had found Sagania. It was bound to make things more difficult for Elizabeth. In practice she was outside the law, but even for the President of Starflight Incorporated there were limits to how far she could go in full view of the mass television audience – and Garamond was going to be a public figure. A rigged trial, with witnesses primed to swear Harald's death had been the result of wilful action, would destroy Garamond. It would, however, focus the world's attention on him even more firmly and help deny Elizabeth the personal revenge she had never been known to forgo. If he and his family were to die it would probably have to appear accidental. And even the most carefully planned accidents could be prevented, if not indefinitely, at least for a reasonable length of time. The future still looked dangerous, but its uncompromising blackness had been alleviated to some extent.

*

Maintaining its height above the surface of the sphere, the *Bissendorf* – which had been closing with the immense fleet at a combined speed of almost two hundred thousand kilometres an hour – swung out of the equatorial plane. It described a wide semicircle around the ships and approached them from the opposite direction, carefully matching velocities until it shared approximately the same parking orbit. In the latter stages of the manoeuvre, telescopic observations by Chief Astronomer Yamoto revealed that several of the vessels at the centre of the swarm were shining by reflected light. He deduced that there was a beam of sunlight being emitted from an aperture in the surface of the sphere, and reported to Garamond accordingly. Shortly afterwards the aperture revealed itself in the telescopes as a thin line of faint light which gradually opened to a narrow ellipse as the *Bissendorf* crept closer.

The big ship's central command gallery took on a crowded appearance as officers who were not on duty found reasons to stay near the curving array of consoles. They were waiting for the first transmissions from the surveillance torpedo which had been dispatched towards the spaceships illuminated by the column of light escaping from Pengelly's Star. There was an atmosphere of tension which made everyone on board the *Bissendorf* aware of how uneventful all their previous wanderings in the galaxy had been.

'I'm not used to this excitement,' Napier whispered. 'Round about this stage on a trip I'm usually tucked away quietly with a bottle of ninety-proof consolation, and I almost think I liked it better that way.'

'I didn't,' Garamond said firmly. 'This is changing things for all of us.'

'I know – I was kidding. Have you tried to work out what the prize money ought to be if it turns out that all these ships can still be flown?'

'No.' Garamond had finished his third bulb of coffee and was bending over to put it in the disposal chute.

'Forget it,' Napier said, with a new note in his voice. 'Look at that, Vance!'

There was a murmur of shock from the central gallery as Garamond was raising his head to look at the first images coming back from the distant torpedo. They were of a large grey ship which had been ripped open along its length like a gutted fish. Twisted sections of infrastructure were visible inside the wound, like entrails. Lesser scars which had not penetrated the hull criss-crossed the remainder of the great ovoid's sunlit side.

'Something really chopped her up.'

'Not as much as the next one.'

The images were changing rapidly as the surveillance torpedo, unhampered by any considerations of the effects of G-force on human tissue, darted towards a second ship, which proved to be only half a ship. It had been sliced in two, laterally, by some unimaginable weapon, sculpted ripples of metal flowing back from the sheared edges. A small vessel, corresponding in size to a lifeboat, hung in space near the open cross-section, joined to the mother ship by cables.

After the first startled comments a silence fell over the control gallery as the images of destruction were multiplied. An hour passed as the torpedo examined all the ships in the single shaft of sunlight and spiralled outwards into the darkness to scan others by the light of its own flares. It became evident that every vessel in the huge swarm had died violently, cataclysmically. Garamond found that the ships illuminated dimly by the flares were the most hideous – their ruptured hulls, silent, brooding over gashes filled with the black blood of shadow, could have been organic remains, preserved by the chill of space, contorted by ancient agonies.

'A signal has just come up from telemetry,' Napier said. 'There's a malfunctioning developing in the torpedo's flare circuits. Do you want another one sent out?'

'No. I think we've seen enough for the present. Have the torpedo come round and take a look through the aperture. I'm sure Mister Yamoto would like some readings on the sun in there.' Garamond leaned back in his seat and looked at Napier. 'Has it ever struck you as odd that we, as representatives of a warlike race, don't carry any armament?'

61

'It has never come up – the Lindstroms wouldn't want their own ships destroyed by each other. Besides, the main ionizing beam would make a pretty effective weapon.'

'Not in that class.' Garamond nodded at the viewscreens. 'We couldn't even aim it without turning the whole ship.'

'You think those hulls prove Serra's theory about the sphere being a defence?'

'Perhaps.' Garamond's voice was thoughtful. 'We won't know for sure until we have a look inside the sphere and see if there was anything worth defending.'

'What makes you think you would see anything?'

'That.' Garamond pointed at the screen which had just begun to show the new images being transmitted back from the torpedo. The aperture in the dark surface of the sphere was circular and almost a kilometre in diameter. A yellow Sol-type sun hung within it, perfectly centred by the torpedo's aiming mechanisms, and the remarkable thing was that the space inside the sphere did not appear black, as the watchers on board the *Bissendorf* knew it ought to do. It was as blue as the summer skies of Earth.

*

Two hours later, and against all the regulations concerning the safety of Starflight commanders, Garamond was at the head of a small expedition which entered the sphere. The buggy was positioned almost on the edge of the aperture, held in place against the surface by the thrust of its tubes. Garamond was able to grip the strut of a landing leg with one hand and slide the other over the edge of the aperture. Its hard rim was only a few centimetres thick. There was a spongy resistance to the passage of his hand, which told of a force field spanning the aperture like a diaphragm, then his gloved fingers gripped something which felt like grass. He pulled himself through to the inside of the sphere and stood up.

And there – on the edge of a circular black lake of stars, suited and armoured to withstand the lethal vacuum of interplanetary space – Garamond had his first look at the green and infinite meadows of Orbitsville.

seven

Garamond's sense of dislocation was almost complete.

He received an impression of grasslands and low hills running on for ever – and, although his mind was numbed, his thoughts contained an element of immediate acceptance, as if an event for which he had been preparing all his life had finally occurred. Garamond felt as though he had been born again. In that first moment, when his vision was swamped by the brilliance of the impossible landscape, he was able to look at the circular lake of blackness from which he had emerged and see it through alien eyes. The grass – the tall, lush grass grew right to the rim! – shimmered green and it was difficult to accept that there were stars down in that pool. It was impossible to comprehend that were he to lie at its edge and look downwards he would see sunken ships drifting in the black crystal waters . . .

Something was emerging from the lake. Something white, groping blindly upwards.

Garamond's identity returned to him abruptly as he recognized the spacesuited figure of Lieutenant Kraemer struggling to an upright position. He moved to help the other man and became aware of yet another 'impossibility' – there was gravity sufficient to give him almost his normal Earth weight. Kraemer and he leaned against each other like drunk men, bemused, stunned, helpless because there were blue skies where there should have been only the hostile blackness of space, because they had stepped through the looking glass into a secret garden. The grass moved gently, reminding Garamond of perhaps the greatest miracle of all, of the presence of an atmosphere. He felt an insane but powerful urge to open his helmet, and was fighting it when his tear-blurred eyes focused on the buildings.

They were visible at several points around the rim of the aperture, ancient buildings, low and ruinous. The reason they had not registered immediately with Garamond was that time had robbed them of the appearance of artifacts, clothing the shattered walls with moss and climbing grasses. As he began to orient himself within the new reality, and the images being transmitted from eyes to brain became capable of interpretation, he saw amid the ruins the skeletons of what had once been great machines.

'Look over there,' he said. 'What do you think?'

There was no reply from Kraemer. Garamond glanced at his companion, saw his lips moving silently behind his faceplate and remembered they were still on radio communication. Both men switched to the audio circuits which used small microphones and speakers on the chest panels.

'The suit radios seem to have packed up,' Kraemer said casually, then his professional composure cracked. 'Is it a dream? Is it? Is it a dream?' His voice was hoarse.

'If it is, we're all in it together. What do you think of the ruins over there?'

Kraemer shielded his eyes and studied the buildings, apparently seeing them for the first time. 'They remind me of fortifications.'

'Me too.' Garamond's mind made an intuitive leap. 'It wasn't always possible to stroll in here the way we just did.'

'All those dead ships?'

'I'd say a lot of people once tried to come through that opening, and other people tried to keep them out.'

'But why should they? I mean, if the whole inside of the sphere is like this . . .' Kraemer gestured at the sea of grass. 'Oh, Christ! If it's all like this there's as much living room as you'd get on a million Earths.'

'More,' Garamond told him. 'I've already done the sums. This sphere has a surface area equivalent to 625,000,000 times the total surface of Earth. If we allow for the fact that only a quarter of the Earth's surface is land and perhaps only half of that is usable, it means the sphere is equivalent to five billion Earths.

'That's one each for every man, woman and child in existence.'

'Provided one thing.'

'What's that?'

'That we can breathe the air.'

'We'll find that out right now.' Garamond felt a momentary dizziness. When he had been playing around with comparisons of the size of Earth and the sphere he had treated it as a purely mathematical exercise, his mind solely on the figures, but Kraemer had gone ahead of him to think in terms of people actually living on the sphere, arriving at the aperture in fleets sent from crowded and worn-out Earth, spreading outward across those prairies which promised to go on for ever. Trying to accommodate the vision along with his other speculations about the origins and purpose of the sphere brought Garamond an almost-physical pain behind his eyes. And superimposed on all his swirling thoughts, overriding every other consideration, a new concept of his personal status was struggling to be born. If he, Vance Garamond, gave humanity five billion Earths . . . then *he,* and not Elizabeth Lindstrom, would be the most important human being alive . . . then his wife and child would be safe.

'There's an analyser kit in the buggy,' Kraemer said. 'Shall I go for it?'

'Of course.' Garamond was surprised by the lieutenant's question, then with a flash of insight he understood that it had taken only a few minutes of exposure to the unbounded *lebensraum* of the sphere to alter a relationship which was part of the tight, closed society of the Two Worlds. Kraemer was actually reluctant to leave the secret garden by climbing down into the circular black lake, and – as the potential owner of a supercontinent – he saw no reason why Garamond should not go instead. *So quickly,* Garamond thought. *We'll all be changed so quickly.*

Aloud he said, 'While you're getting the kit you can break the news to the others – they'll want to see for themselves.'

'Right.' Kraemer looked pleased at the idea of being first with the most sensational story of all time. He went to the edge of the aperture, lay down and lowered his head into the blackness, obviously straining to force the helmet through the membrane field which retained the sphere's atmosphere. After wriggling sideways a little to obtain his grip on the buggy's leg, Kraemer slid out of sight into the darkness. Garamond again felt a sense of dislocation. The fact that he had weight, that there was a natural-seeming gravity pulling him 'downwards' against the grassy soil created an illusion that he was standing on the surface of a planet. His instincts rebelled against the idea that he was standing on a thin shell of unknown metal, that below him was the hard vacuum of space, that the buggy was close underneath his feet, upside down, clinging to the sphere by the force of its drive.

Garamond moved away from the aperture a short distance, shocked by the incongruity of the heavy spacesuit which shut him off from what surely must be his natural element. He knelt for a closer look at the grass. It grew thickly, in mixed varieties which to his inexperienced eye had stems and laminae very similar to those of Earth. He parted the grass, pushed his gloved fingers into the matted roots and scooped up a handful of brown soil. Small crumbs of it clung to the material of his gloves, making moist smears. Garamond looked upwards and for the first time noticed the lacy white streamers of cloud. With the small sun positioned vertically overhead it was difficult to study the sky, but beyond the cloud he thought he could distinguish narrow bands of a lighter blue which created a delicate ribbed effect curving from horizon to horizon. He made a mental note to point it out to Chief Science Officer O'Hagan for early investigation, and returned his attention to the soil. Digging down into it a short distance he came to the ubiquitous grey metal of the shell, its surface unmarked by the damp earth. Garamond placed his hand against the metal and tried to imagine the building of the sphere, to visualize the creation of a seamless globe of metal with a circumference of a billion kilometres.

There could be only one source for such an inconceivable quantity of shell material, and that was in the sun itself. Matter is energy, and energy is matter. Every active star hurls the equivalent of millions of tons a day of its own substance into space in the form of

*light and other radiations. But in the case of Pengelly's Star some-
one had set up a boundary, turned that energy back on itself,
manipulating and modifying it, translating it into matter. With
precise control over the most elemental forces of the universe they
had created an impervious shell of exactly the sort of material they
wanted – harder than diamond, immutable, eternal. When the
sphere was complete, grown to the required thickness, they had
again dipped their hands into the font of energy and wrought fresh
miracles, coating the interior surface of the sphere with soil and
water and air. Organic acids, even complete cells and seeds, had
been constructed in the same way, because at the ultimate level of
reality there is no difference between a blade of grass and one of
steel . . .*

'The air is good, sir.' Kraemer's voice came from close behind.
Garamond stood up, turned and saw the lieutenant had opened
his faceplate.

'What was the reading like?'

'A shade low in oxygen, but everything else is about right.'
Kraemer was grinning like a schoolboy. 'You should try some.'

'I will.' Garamond opened his own helmet and took a deep
breath. The air was soft and thick and pure. He discovered at
that moment that he had never known truly fresh air before.
Low shouts came from the direction of the aperture as other
spacesuited figures emerged.

'I told the others they could come through,' Kraemer said.
'All except Braunek – he's holding the buggy in place. It's all
right, isn't it?'

'It's all right, yes. I'll be setting up a rota system to let everybody on the ship have a look before we go back.' Again Garamond sensed a difference in Kraemer's attitude – before the
lieutenant had seen the interior of the sphere he would not have
cleared the buggy without obtaining permission.

'Before we go back? But as soon as we signal Earth the traffic's
all going to be coming this way. Why go back?'

'No reason, I suppose.' Garamond had been thinking about
Aileen's reluctance ever to travel more than a few kilometres
from their apartment. He had been planning to return her to

the old familiar surroundings as soon as possible, but perhaps there was no need. Standing on the interior surface of the sphere was as close as one could get to being on the infinite plane of the geometer, yet there was nothing in the experience to inspire agoraphobia. The line of sight did not tangent away from the downward curve of a planet and so the uniform density of the air set a limit to the distance a man could see. Garamond studied the horizon. It appeared to curve upwards slightly, in contrast to that of Earth, but it did not seem much further away. There was no sense of peering into immensities.

Kraemer put the toe of one boot down into the small hole Garamond had made and tapped the metal at the bottom. 'Did you find anything?'

'Such as?'

'Circuits. For this synthetic gravity.'

'No. I don't think we'll find any circuits in our sense of the word.'

'What then?'

'Atoms with their interiors rearranged or specially designed to do a job. Perfect machines.'

'It sounds incredible.'

'We've taken the first step in that direction ourselves with our magnetic resonance engines. Anyway, what could be more incredible than all this?' Some instinct prompted Garamond to push the soil back into the hole and tamp it down with his foot, repairing the damage he had done to the grassy surface. In the region close to the aperture the soil was thinly distributed, but there were hills in the distance which looked as though they could have been formed by drifting.

'As soon as your men have got over the shock tell them to gather vegetation and soil samples,' he said.

'I already have,' Kraemer replied carelessly. 'By the way – none of the suit radios is working, though mine was all right again when I went back out through the aperture.'

'There must be a damping effect – that's something else for O'Hagan to investigate when he gets here. Let's have a look at some of those ruins.'

They walked to the nearest of the indistinct mounds. Under the blanket of climbing grasses there was just enough remaining structure to suggest a floor plan of massive walls and simple square rooms. Here and there, close to the black lake of stars, were distorted metallic stumps which had once been parts of machines. They had a sagging, lava-flow appearance as though they had been destroyed by intense heat.

Kraemer gave a low whistle. 'Who do you think won? The people who were trying to get in, or the ones who were trying to keep them out?'

'I'd say the invaders won, Lieutenant. I've been thinking about all those dead ships hanging out there. They can't be in their battle stations because even if they had been stationary during the fight the forces used against them would have kicked them adrift and there would have been nothing for us to find. It looks as though they were rounded up and carefully parked just outside the aperture.'

'Why?'

'For salvage, perhaps. There may be no metals available within the sphere.'

'For beating into ploughshares? It's good farming country, all right – but where are the farmers?'

'Nomads? Perhaps you don't have to till the soil. Maybe you just keep moving for ever, following the seasons, with the grain always ripening just ahead of you.'

Kraemer laughed. 'What seasons? It must always be high summer here – and high noon, too. It can't even get dark with that sun right above your head.'

'But it *is* getting dark, Lieutenant.' Garamond spoke peacefully, all capacity for surprise exhausted. 'Look over there.'

He pointed at the horizon beyond the black ellipse of the aperture to where the shimmering blue-greens of the distance had begun to deepen. There was an unmistakable gathering of shade.

'That's impossible,' Kraemer protested. He looked up at the sun. 'Oh, no!'

Garamond looked up and saw that the sun was no longer

circular. It had one straight side, like a gold coin from which somebody had clipped a generous segment. Shouts from the other men indicated that they had noticed the event. While they watched, the still-brilliant area of the sun's disc grew progressively smaller as though a shutter were being drawn across it. At the same time, keeping pace, the darkness increased on the corresponding horizon and a new phenomenon made itself apparent. The delicate ribbed effect which Garamond had noticed in the sky earlier became clearer, the alternating bands of lighter and darker blue now standing out vividly. In the space of a minute, as the sun began to disappear completely, the slim curving ribs became the dominant feature of the sky, swirling across it from two foci, sharply defined as the striations in polished agate. Near the horizon, where they dipped behind denser levels of air, the bands blurred and dispersed into a prismatic haze. The last searing sliver of sun vanished and Garamond glimpsed a wall of shadow rushing over the landscape towards him at orbital speed, then it was night, beneath a canopy of stratified sapphire.

Garamond stayed beside the lake of stars for an hour before returning to his ship and sending a tachyonic signal to Starflight House.

eight

It was almost exactly four months later that Elizabeth Lindstrom's flagship took up its station outside the sphere's entrance.

*

Garamond had spent part of the time carrying out investigations into Orbitsville – the name for the sphere had originated with an unknown crew member – but, as it was primarily equipped for locate-and-report missions, the *Bissendorf* did not carry a large science team, and the studies were necessarily limited. The astronomy section, under Sammy Yamoto, made the most profound discovery of all – that there was yet another sphere surrounding Pengelly's Star.

It was smaller than Orbitsville, non-material in nature yet capable of reflecting or deflecting the sun's outpourings of light and heat. Yamoto described it as a 'globular filigree of force fields', a phrase of which he appeared inordinately proud, judging by the frequency with which it was used in his reports. Of the inner sphere's surface area, precisely half was made up of narrow strips, effectively opaque, curving in a general north-south direction. Their function was to cast great moving bars of shadow on the grasslands of Orbitsville, producing the alternating periods of light and darkness, day and night, without which plant life could not survive. Yamoto was not able to observe the inner sphere directly, but he could chart its structure by studying the bands of light and darkness as they moved across the far side of Orbitsville, 320 million kilometres away in the 'night' sky. And he was able to show that the shadow sphere not only created night and day but was also responsible for a progression of seasons. In one quarter of the sphere, corresponding to winter, the opaque night-producing strips were wider and therefore separated by narrower gaps of light; at the opposite side the strips were reduced in width to engender the shorter nights and longer days of summer.

To facilitate Yamoto's work a small plastic observatory was prefabricated in the *Bissendorf*'s workshops and transferred to a site within Orbitsville. Several more buildings were added as other sections found reason to prolong their work in the interior, and the nucleus of a scientific colony was formed.

A substantial portion of the effort was put into trying to solve the annoying riddle of why no radio communicator would work inside the sphere. At first it was anticipated that a simple solution and practical remedy would be found, but the weeks slipped by without any progress being made. It appeared that the equally inexplicable synthetic gravity field was responsible for damping out all electromagnetic radiation. In an effort to get new data on the possible mechanics of the phenomenon, O'Hagan's team took a photographic torpedo and gave it enough extra thrust to enable it to take off from the inner surface of Orbitsville. The purpose of the experiment was to measure the gravity gradient and to see if the radio guidance and telemetry systems would operate if the signals were travelling at right angles to the surface. After a flawless programmed start, the torpedo began tracing random patterns in the sky and made a programmed automatic landing several kilometres away from the aperture. Pessimists began to predict that the only long-range communication possible on Orbitsville would be by modulation of light beams.

Another discovery was that the utterly inert and incredibly hard shell of the sphere was impervious to all radiation except gravity waves. The latter were able to pass through, otherwise the star system's outer planet would have tangented off towards interstellar space, but not even the most energetic particles entered Orbitsville from the outer universe, except by means of the aperture. Certain peculiarities in the measurements of radiation levels from Pengelly's Star itself led O'Hagan to give Garamond a confidential report in which he suggested that flickerwing ships might not be able to operate within the sphere, due to lack of available reaction mass. The subject was earmarked for priority investigation by the fully equipped teams which would arrive later.

Garamond received an increasing number of requests from crewmen, especially those who were inactive when the main drive was not in use, for permission to stay on Orbitsville under canvas. At first he encouraged the idea, but Napier reported that the remaining personnel were becoming resentful of their relaxed and sunburned colleagues whose eyes held a new kind of contentment and surety when they returned to ship duties. Partly to combat the divisive forces, Garamond took the *Bissendorf* on a circuit of Orbitsville's equatorial plane and established that no other entrances were visible.

He also set teams of men to work on moving the swarm of dead ships to a position a thousand kilometres down orbit from the aperture. With the ships at their new station, photographic teams went inside as many as was practicable and made records of their findings. They confirmed Garamond's first guess that the hulls had been used as mines and sources of supply. The interiors were gutted, stripped to the bare metal of their hulls, and in some cases it turned out that what had first been thought of as the havoc of battle was actually the work of scavengers. An unfortunate by-product was that virtually nothing was found which would have let researchers deduce the appearance of the aliens who had built and flown the huge fleet. The most significant find was a section of metal staircase and handrailing which hinted that the aliens had been bipeds of about the same size as humans.

Where were they now?

The question came in for more discussion than did speculations on the whereabouts of the beings who had created Orbitsville. It was understood that the sphere-builders had possessed a technology of an entirely different order to that of the race which had produced the ships. The instinctive belief was that the sphere-builders were unknowable, that they had moved on to new adventures or new phases of their existence, because it would be impossible to be near them without their presence being felt. Orbitsville appeared to be and was accepted as a gift from the galactic past.

Garamond brought Aileen and Christopher into the sphere, through the newly constructed L-shaped entrance port, for a strangely peaceful vacation. Aileen was, as he had predicted, able to adjust to Orbitsville's up-curving horizons without any psychological upsets, and Chris took to it like a foal turned loose in spring pastures. In the daytime Garamond watched the boy's skin acquire the gold of the new-found sun, and at nights he sat outside with Aileen beneath the fabulous archways of the sky, their gratification all the more intense because of the period of despair which had preceded it.

Only in dreams, or in the half-world between consciousness and sleep, did Garamond feel any apprehension at the thought of Elizabeth advancing across the light-years which lay between Orbitsville and Earth.

*

To the unaided vision it would have appeared that her flagship came alone, but in fact it was at the head of a fleet of seventy vessels. An interstellar ramjet on maindrive was surrounded by its intake field, a vast insubstantial maw with an area of up to half a million square kilometres, and for this reason the closest formation ever flown was in the form of a thousand-kilometre grid. The fleet was unwieldy even by Starflight standards. It spent two days in matching velocities with the galactic drift of Pengelly's Star and in deploying its individual units in parking orbit. When each ship had been accurately positioned and its electromagnetic wings furled, the flagship – *Starflier IV* – advanced slowly on ion drive until it was almost alongside the *Bissendorf*. Captain Vance Garamond received a formal invitation to go on board.

The very act of donning the black-and-silver dress uniform, for the first time ever in the course of a mission, made him aware that once again he was within Elizabeth's sphere of influence. He was not conscious of any fear – Orbitsville had had too profound an effect on the situation for that – yet he was filled with a vague distaste each time he thought of the forthcoming interview. For the past four months he had been certain of the fact that Elizabeth's consequence had been reduced to normal human dimensions, but her arrival at the head of an armada suggested that the old order was still a reality. For her, the only reality.

The sight of his dress uniform had disturbed Aileen, too. As the doors of the transit dock opened and the little buggy ventured out on to the black ocean of space, Garamond remembered the way his wife had kissed him before he left. She had been abstracted, almost cold, and had turned away quickly. It was as though she were suppressing all emotion, but in his final glimpse of her she had been holding their golden snail against her cheek. He stood behind the pilot of the buggy for the whole of the short trip, watching the flagship expand until it filled the forward screens. When the docking manoeuvre had been completed he stepped watchfully but confidently into the transit bay where a group of Starflight officials were waiting. Behind the officials were a number of men in civilian dress and carrying scene recorders. With a minimum of ceremony Garamond was escorted to the Presidential suite and ushered into the principal stateroom. Elizabeth must have given previous instructions, because his escorts withdrew immediately and in silence.

The President was standing with her back to the door. She was wearing a long close-fitting gown of white satin – her favourite style of dress – and three white spaniels floated drowsily in the air close to her feet. Garamond was shocked to see that Elizabeth had lost most of her hair. The thinning black strands clung to her scalp in patches, making her look old and diseased. She continued to stand with her back to him although she must have been aware of his presence.

'My Lady . . .' Garamond scuffed the floor with his magnetic-soled boots, and the President slowly turned around. The skin of her small-chinned face was pale and glistening.

'Why did you do it, Captain?' Her voice was low. 'Why did you run from me?'

'My Lady, I . . .' Garamond, unprepared for a direct question, was lost for words.

'Why were you afraid of me?'

'I panicked. What happened to your son was a pure accident – he fell when I wasn't even near him – but I panicked. And I ran.' It occurred to Garamond that Elizabeth might have sound political and tactical reasons for choosing to meet him as a mother who had lost a child rather than as an empress in danger of being usurped, but it did not lessen her advantage.

Incredibly, Elizabeth smiled her asymmetrical, knowing smile. 'You thought I wouldn't understand, that I might lash out at you.'

'It would have been a natural reaction.'

'You shouldn't have been afraid of me, Captain.'

'I . . . I'm glad.' *This is fantastic,* Garamond thought numbly. *She doesn't believe any of it. I don't believe any of it. So why go on with the charade?*

'. . . suffered, and you've suffered,' Elizabeth was saying. 'I think we always will, but I want you to know that I bear you no grudge.' She came closer to him, still smiling, and her soft satiny abdomen brushed his knuckles. Garamond thought of spiders.

'There isn't any way I can express how sorry I am that the accident occurred.'

'I know.' Elizabeth's voice was gentle, but suddenly the room was filled with her sweet, soupy odour and Garamond knew that, just for an instant, she had thought of killing him.

'My Lady, if this is too much for you . . .'

Her face hardened instantly. 'What makes you think so?'

'Nothing.'

'Very well, then. We have important business matters to discuss, Captain. Did you know that the Council, with my consent, has authorized the payment to you of ten million monits?'

Garamond shook his head. 'Ten million?'

'Yes. Does that seem a lot of money to you?'

'It seems all the money there is.'

Elizabeth laughed and turned away from him, disturbing the spaniels in their airborne slumbers. 'It's nothing, Captain. *Nothing!* You will, of course, be appointed to the council I'm setting up to advise on the development and exploitation of Lindstromland, and your salary from that alone will be two million monits a year. Then there's . . .' Elizabeth paused.

'What's the matter, Captain? You look surprised.'

'I am.'

'At the size of your salary? Or the fact that the sphere has been officially named after my family?'

'The name of the sphere is unimportant,' Garamond said stonily, too disturbed by what Elizabeth had said to think about exhibiting the proper degree of deference. 'What is important is that it can't be controlled and exploited. You sounded as if you were planning to parcel up the land and sell it in the same way that Terranova is handled.'

'We don't sell plots on Terranova – they are given freely, through Government-controlled agencies.'

'To anybody who can pay the Starflight transportation charge. It's the same thing.'

'Really?' Elizabeth examined Garamond through narrowed eyes. 'You're an expert on such matters, are you?'

'I don't need to be. The facts are easily understood.' Garamond felt he was rushing towards a dangerous precipice, but he had no desire to hold back.

'In that case you'll make an excellent council member – all the others regard the Starflight operation as being extremely complex.'

'In practice,' Garamond said doggedly. 'But not in principle.'

Elizabeth gave her second unexpected smile of the interview. 'In principle, then, why can't Lindstromland be developed in the normal way?'

'For the same reason that water-sellers can make a living only in the desert.'

'You mean where there's a lot of water freely available nobody will pay for it.'

'No doubt that sounds childishly simple to you, My Lady, but it's what I meant.'

'I'm intrigued by your thought processes, Captain.' Elizabeth was giving no sign of being angered by Garamond's attitude. 'How can you compare selling water and opening up a new world?'

Garamond gave a short laugh. 'Yours are the intriguing thought processes if you're comparing Orbitsville to an ordinary planet.'

'Orbitsville?'

'Lindstromland. It isn't like an ordinary planet.'

'I'm aware of the difference in size.'

'You aren't.'

Elizabeth's tolerance began to fade. 'Be careful about what you say, Captain.'

'With respect, My Lady, you aren't aware of the difference in size. Nobody is, and nobody ever will be. *I'm* not aware of it, and I've flown right round Orbitsville.'

'Surely the fact that you were able to . . .'

'I was travelling at a hundred thousand kilometres an hour,' Garamond said in a steady voice. 'At that speed I could have orbited Earth in twenty-five minutes. Do you know how long it took to get round Orbitsville ? *Forty-two days!*'

'I grant you we're dealing with a new order of magnitude.'

'And that's only a linear comparison. Don't you see there's just no way you can handle the amount of living space involved ?'

Elizabeth shrugged. 'I've already told you that Starflight doesn't concern itself with the apportionment of land, so the exact area of Lindstromland is of no concern to us. We will, of course, continue to make a fair profit from our transportation services.'

'But that's the whole point,' Garamond said angrily. 'Even if it wasn't a disguised land charge, the transportation fee should be abolished.'

'Why ?'

'Because we now have all the land we can use. In those circumstances it is intolerable that there should be any kind of economic brake on the natural and instinctive flow of people towards the new land.'

'You, of all people, should know that there's nothing natural or instinctive about building and sailing a flickerwing ship.' A rare tinge of colour was appearing in Elizabeth's waxy cheeks. 'It can't be done without money.'

Garamond shook his head. 'It can't be done without *people*. A culture which had never developed the concept of money, or property, could cross space just as well as we do.'

'At last !' Elizabeth took two quick steps towards Garamond, then stopped, swaying in magnetic shoes. 'At last I know you, Captain. If money is so distasteful to you, I take it you are refusing a place on the development council ?'

'I am.'

'And your bounty ? Ten million monits taken from the pockets of the people of the Two Worlds. You're refusing that, too ?'

'I'm refusing that, too.'

'You're too late,' Elizabeth snapped, savouring a triumph which only she understood. 'It has already been credited to your account.'

'I'll return it to you.'

Elizabeth shook her head decisively. 'No, Captain. You're a very famous man back on the Two Worlds – and I must be seen to give you everything you deserve. Now, return to your ship.'

On the way back to the *Bissendorf*, Garamond's mind was filled with the President's admission that he had become too important to be disposed of like any other human being. *And yet*, came the disturbing thought, *there had been that look of satisfaction in her eyes.*

nine

The new house allocated for Garamond's use was a rectangular, single-storey affair. It was one of several dozen built from plastic panels which had been prefabricated in a Starflight workshop on board one of Elizabeth's ships.

The compact structure was situated less than two kilometres from the aperture to the outside universe, where the coating of soil was still thin, and so was held in place by suction pads which gripped the underlying metal of the shell. After a matter of days living in it Garamond found that he could forget about the hard vacuum of space beginning only a few centimetres below his living-room floor. The furnishings were sparse but comfortable, and a full range of colour projectors and entertainment machines – plus an electronic tutor for Christopher – gave it something of the atmosphere of a luxury week-end lodge.

There was an efficient kitchen supplied with provisions from shipboard stores in the early stages, but the expectation was that the colonists would become self-supporting as regards food within a year. It was late summer in that part of Orbitsville and the edible grasses were approaching a tawny ripeness. Even before a systemized agriculture could be established to produce grain harvests, the grass would be fully utilized – part of it synthetically digested to create protein foods, the rest yielding cellulose for the production of a range of acetate plastics.

Garamond was technically still in command of the *Bissendorf*, but he spent much of his time in the house, telling himself he was helping his family to put down roots. In reality he was trying to cope with the sense of having been cut adrift. He acquired the habit of standing at a window which faced the aperture and watching the ever-increasing tempo of activity at the Starflight out post. Machinery, vehicles, supplies of all kinds came through the L-shaped entry tubes in a continuous stream; new buildings were erected every day amid moraines of displaced soil; a skein of dirt roads wound around and through the complex, with its loose ends straggling off into the grasslands. Earth's beachhead was becoming well established, and as it did so Garamond felt more and more redundant.

'The weirdest thing about it is that I feel possessive,' he said to his wife. 'I keep lecturing people about the inconceivable size of Orbitsville, telling them it couldn't be controlled by a thousand Starflight corporations – yet I have a gut-feeling it's my personal property. I guess that in a way I'm as much out of touch with reality as Liz Lindstrom.'

Aileen shook her head. 'You're angry at the way she's proposing to handle things.'

'Angry at myself.'

'Why?'

'What made me think Starflight House would quietly bow out of existence to make way for a publicly-funded transportation system? From what I hear, Liz's public relations teams are plugging the notion that Starflight already *is* a semi-governmental concern. That was a hard one to put over when there was just Terranova and the amount of land a settler got was determined by how much he paid for his passage, but now it's different.'

'In what way?' Aileen looked up from the boy's shirt she was hand-stitching. Her deeply tanned face was sympathetic but unconcerned – since arriving on Orbitsville she had developed a peaceful optimism. It seemed that the principal element of his wife's personality, her unremarkable pleasantness, was standing her in good stead in the alien environment.

'There's to be a standard transportation charge and no limitation to the amount of land a settler can occupy. That will make the operation seem pretty altruistic to most people. The trouble is it's easy to see how they would get that impression.'

Since turning down membership of Elizabeth's development council Garamond had found it difficult to keep himself informed of her activities, but he could visualize the approach she was using to sell Orbitsville on overcrowded Earth. The newly-established fact that the volume of space within the sphere was totally free of hydrogen or other matter, ruling out the use of flickerwing ships, could even be turned to Starflight's advantage. It was likely that a very long time would elapse before the unwieldy and inefficient type of ship which carried its own reaction mass could be redeveloped sufficiently to make any impression on the five billion Earth-areas available within the sphere. Orbitsville, then, was truly the ultimate frontier, a place where a man and his family could load up a solar-powered vehicle with supplies, plus an 'iron cow' to convert grass into food, and drive off into a green infinity. The life offered would be simple, and perhaps hard – in many ways similar to that of a pioneer in the American West – but in the coast-to-coast *urbs* of Earth there was a great yearning for just that kind of escape. The risk of dying of overwork or simple appendicitis on a lonely farm hundreds of light-years from Earth was infinitely preferable to the prospect of going down in a food riot in Paris or Melbourne. No matter how much Starflight charged for passage to Orbitsville, there would always be more than enough people to fill the big ships.

'Does the President have to be altruistic?' Aileen said, and Garamond knew that she was drawing comparisons between Liz Lindstrom and herself, between a woman who had unexpectedly lost a son and one whose husband and child had been reprieved. 'What's wrong with making a reasonable percentage on services rendered?'

'In this case – everything.' Garamond suppressed a pang of annoyance. 'Don't you see that? Look, Earth has been raped and polluted and choked to death, but right here on Orbitsville there's room for every human being there is to lose himself for ever. We've made all the mistakes and learned all the lessons back on Earth, and now we've been given this chance to start off from scratch again. The whole situation demands an almost complete transfer of population – and it could be done, Aileen. At our level of technology it could be done, but the entire Starflight operation is based on it *not* being done!

'In order for Elizabeth to go on making her quote reasonable percentage unquote there has to be a potential, a high population pressure on Earth and a low one elsewhere. I wouldn't be surprised if it turned out that the Lindstroms are behind the failure of all the main population control programmes.'

'That's ridiculous, Vance.' Aileen began to laugh.

'Is it?' Garamond turned away from the window, mollified by his wife's evident happiness. 'Maybe so, but you don't hear them complaining much about the birth rate.'

'Talking about birth rates – our own has been pretty static for a long time.' Aileen caught his hand and held it against her cheek. 'Wouldn't you like to be the father of the first child born on Orbitsville?'

'I'm not sure, but it's impossible anyway. The first shiploads of settlers are on their way, and – from what I've heard about the Terranova run – a lot of the women always arrive pregnant. It's something to do with the lack of recreational facilities on the journey.'

'How about the first one conceived on Orbitsville then?'

'That's more like it.' Garamond knelt beside his wife's chair, took her in his arms and they kissed.

Aileen drew back from him after a few seconds. 'You'll have to do better than that.'

'I'm sorry. I keep thinking about the people, beings or gods – whatever you want to call them – who built Orbitsville.'

'Who doesn't?'

'I don't understand them.'

'Who does?'

'You know, there's enough living space in Orbitsville to support every intelligent being in the galaxy. For all we know, that's why it was created, and yet ...'

Garamond allowed his voice to die away. He suspected Aileen would accuse him of paranoia if he speculated aloud about why the sphere-builders had created a hostel for an entire galaxy's homeless – and then played into Elizabeth Lindstrom's hands by providing only one entrance.

*

Chick Truman was one of a breed of human beings who had come into existence with the development of interstellar travel. He was a frontiersman-technician. His father and grandfather had helped with the opening up of Terranova and with the initial surveying of a dozen other planets which, although unsuitable for colonization, had some commercial or scientific potential. He had received little in the way of formal technical training but, like all other members of the fraternity of gypsy-engineers, seemed to have an inborn knowledge of the entire range of mechanical skills. It was as though the accumulated experience of generations had begun to produce men for whom the analysis of an electrical circuit or the tuning of an engine was a matter of instinct.

One attribute which distinguished Truman from most of his fellows was a strong, if undisciplined, interest in philosophy. And it was this which had fired his mind as he set up camp on the lower slopes of the hills which ringed Orbitsville's single aperture at a distance of about sixty kilometres. He was half of a two-man team which had been sent out to erect a bank of laser reflectors as part of an experimental communications system. They had reached their target minutes before the wall of darkness had come rushing from the east, and now Truman's partner, Peter Krogt, was busy preparing food and laying out their sleeping bags. Truman himself was concerned with less prosaic matters. He had lit a pipe of tobacco, was comfortably seated with his back to the transporter and was staring into the incredible ribbed archways of the sky at night.

'The Assumption of Mediocrity is a useful philosophical weapon,' he was saying, 'but it can backfire on the guy who uses it. I know that some of the greatest advances in human thought were achieved by assuming there's nothing odd or freakish about our own little patch – that's what set Albert Einstein off.'

'Help me open these containers,' Krogt said.

Without moving, Truman released a cloud of aromatic smoke. 'But consider the case of, say, two beetles living at the bottom of a hole on a golf course. These bugs have never been out of that hole, but if they have a philosophical turn of mind they can describe the rest of the universe just by using available evidence. What would their universe be like, Pete?'

'Who cares?'

'Nice attitude, Pete. Their projected universe would be an infinite series of round holes with big white balls dropping into them during daylight hours.'

Krogt had opened the food containers unaided and he handed one to Truman. 'What are you talking about, Chick?'

'I'm telling you what's wrong with the management back at base. Listen . . . We've been on Orbitsville for months, right?'

'Right.'

'Now take this little jaunt you and I are on right now. These hills are three hundred metres high. Our orders are to set up the reflectors at an elevation of two hundred and fifty metres. We've been told where to set them, where to aim them, what deviation will be acceptable, how long to take with the assignment – but there's one thing we *haven't* been told to do. And I find it a pretty astonishing omission, Pete.'

'Your yeasteak's getting cold.'

'Why did nobody tell us to climb the extra fifty metres to the top of the hill and have a look at the other side?'

'Because there's no need,' Krogt said heavily. 'There's nothing there but grass and scrub. The whole inside of this ball is nothing but prairie.'

'There you go! The Assumption of Mediocrity.'

'It isn't an assumption.' Krogt gestured with his fork towards the shimmering watered-silk canopy of the sky. 'They've had a look around with telescopes.'

'Telescopes!' Truman sneered to cover up the fact that he had forgotten about telescopic examination of the far side of Orbitsville, then his talent for rapid mental calculation came to his aid. 'We're talking about a distance of more than two astronomical units, sonny. If you were standing on Earth, what would one of those spyglasses tell you about life on Mars?'

'More'n I want to know. Are you going to eat this yeasteak or will I?'

'You eat it.'

Truman got to his feet, slightly dismayed at the way in which a discussion on philosophy had led him to renounce his meal, and marched away up the slope. He was breathing heavily by the time he reached the rounded summit and paused to re-light his pipe. The yellow flame from the lighter dazzled his eyes and almost a minute had passed before Truman appreciated that, spread out on the plain below him, dim and peaceful, were the lights of an alien civilization.

ten

The arrival of the first wave of ships had surprised Garamond in two ways – by its timing, which could have been achieved only if it had set out within days of Elizabeth's own arrival on Orbitsville; and by its size. There were eighty Type G2 vessels, each of which carried more than four thousand people. A third of a million settlers, who originally must have been destined for the relatively well-prepared territories of Terranova, had been diverted to a new destination where there was not even a shed to give them shelter for their first night.

'It beats me,' Cliff Napier said, sipping his first coffee of the day. He was off duty and had spent the night in Garamond's house. 'All right, so Terranova has only one usable continent and it's filling up fast, but the situation isn't *that* urgent. No matter how you look at it, these people are going to have a rough time at first. They haven't even got proper transportation.'

'You're wondering why they agreed to come?' Garamond asked, finishing his own coffee.

Napier nodded. 'The average colonist is a family man who doesn't want to expose his wife and kids to more unknown risks than necessary. How did Starflight get them to come here?'

'I'll tell you.' Aileen came into the room with a pot of fresh coffee and began refilling the cups. 'Chris and I were down at the store this morning while you two were still in your beds, and I talked to people who saw the first families disembarking before dawn. You know, you don't learn much by lying around snoring.'

'All right, Aileen, we both think you're wonderful. Now, what are you talking about?'

'They were given free passages,' Aileen said, obviously pleased at being able to impart the news.

Garamond shook his head. 'I don't believe it.'

'It's true, Vance. They say Starflight House is giving free travel to anybody who signs on for Lindstromland within the first six months.'

'It's a trick.'

'Oh, Vance!' Aileen's eyes were reproachful. 'Why don't you admit you were wrong about Elizabeth? Besides, what sort of a trick could it be? What could she hope to gain?'

'It's a trick,' Garamond said stubbornly. 'What she's done isn't even legal – the teams from the Government land agencies haven't got here yet.'

'But you always say the law doesn't mean anything to the Lindstroms.'

'Not when they want to take something. This is different.'

'Now you're being childish,' Aileen snapped.

'He isn't,' Napier said. 'Take our word for it, Aileen – Liz Lindstrom never acts out of character.'

Aileen's face had lost some of its natural colour. 'Oh, you know it all, of course. You know all about how it feels for a woman to lose her only . . .' She stopped speaking abruptly.

'Child,' Garamond finished for her. 'Don't hold anything back for my benefit.'

'I'm sorry. It's just . . .' Lenses of tears magnified Aileen's eyes as she walked out of the room.

The two men finished their coffee in silence, each dwelling on his own thoughts. Garamond wondered if the sense of pointlessness which was silting through his mind was due to his having to stand by helplessly while the President imposed her will on Orbitsville, or if it sprang from the slow realization that he was out of a job. The entire Stellar Exploration Arm had become superfluous because there was no need for the big ships to search the star fields ever again. *Could it be,* he wondered, *that I existed only for the search?*

With an obvious effort at diplomacy, Napier began discussing the work being carried out by the Starflight research teams. Despite the use of more sophisticated and more powerful cutting tools than had been available on board the *Bissendorf* nobody had even managed to scratch the shell material. At the same time, studies of the inner shell were indicating that its movement was not a simple east-west rotation, but that subtle geometries were involved with the object of producing a normal progression of day and night close to the polar areas.

Another team had been working continuously on the diaphragm field which prevented the atmosphere from rushing into space through the kilometre-wide aperture in the outer shell. No significant progress had been made there, either. The force field employed was unlike anything ever generated by human engineers in that it reacted equally against the passage of metallic and non-metallic objects. Observations of the field showed that it was lenticular in shape, being several metres thick at the centre. Unlike the shell material, it was transparent to cosmic rays and actually appeared to refract them – a discovery which had led to the suggestion that, as well as being a sealing device, it was intended to disperse cosmic rays in such a way as to produce a small degree of mutation in Orbitsville's flora and fauna – if the latter existed. In general, the field seemed more amenable than the shell material to investigation because it had proved possible to cause small local alterations in its structure, and to produce temporary leaks by firing beams of electrons through it.

'Interesting stuff, isn't it?' Napier concluded.

'Fascinating,' Garamond said automatically.

'You don't sound convinced. I'm going to have a look at the new arrivals.'

Garamond smiled. 'Okay, Cliff. We'll see you for lunch.'

He got to his feet and was walking to the door with Napier when the communicator set, which had been connected to the central exchange by a landline pending a solution of the radio transmission problem, chimed to announce an incoming call. Garamond pressed the ACCEPT button and the solid image of a heavy-shouldered and prematurely grey young man appeared at the projection focus. He was wearing civilian clothing and his face was unknown to Garamond.

'Good morning, Captain,' the stranger said in a slightly breathless voice. 'I'm Colbert Mason of the Two Worlds News Agency. Have any other reporters been in touch with you?'

'Other reporters? No.'

'Thank God for that – I'm the first,' Mason said fervently.

'The first? I didn't know Starflight had authorized transportation for newsmen.'

'They haven't.' Mason gave a shaky laugh. 'I had to emigrate to this place with my wife more or less permanently, and I know other reporters have done the same thing. I'm just lucky my ship disembarked first. If you'll give me an interview, that is.'

'Have you been off-world before?'

'No, sir. First time, but I'd have gone right round the galaxy for this chance.'

Garamond recognized the flattery but also found himself genuinely impressed by the young newsman. 'What did you want to talk to me about?'

'What did I . . .?' Mason spread his hands helplessly. 'The lot! Anything and everything. Do you know, sir, that back on Earth you're regarded as the most famous man ever? Even if you'd answered the tachygrams we sent you we'd still have considered it worth while to try for a face-to-face interview.'

'Tachygrams? I got no signals from Earth. Hold on a minute.' Garamond killed the audio channel and turned to Napier. 'Elizabeth?'

Napier's heavy-lidded eyes were alert. 'I'd say so. She didn't like your views on how Orbitsville should be handled. In fact, I'm surprised this reporter got through the net. He must have been very smart, or lucky.'

'Let's make him luckier.' Garamond opened the audio circuit again. 'I've got a good story for you, Mason. Are you prepared to run it exactly as I tell it?'

'Of course.'

'Okay. Come straight out to my place.'

'I can't, sir. I called you because I think I'm being watched, and there may not be much time.'

'All right, then. You can report that in my opinion the potential of Orbitsville is . . .'

'Orbitsville?'

'The local name for Lindstromland . . .' Garamond stopped speaking as the image of the reporter broke up into motes of coloured light which swarmed in the air for a second before abruptly vanishing. He waited for the image to re-establish itself but nothing happened.

'I thought it was too good to be true,' Napier commented. 'Somebody pulled out the plug on you.'

'I know. Where do you think Mason was speaking from?'

'Must have been from one of the depot stores. Those are the only places where he'd have any access to a communicator set.'

'Let's get down there right now.' Garamond pulled on a lightweight jacket and, without waiting to explain to Aileen, hurried from the house into Orbitsville's changeless noon. Christopher looked up from the solitary game he was playing in the grass but did not speak. Garamond waved to the boy and strode out in the direction of the clustered buildings around the aperture.

'It's bloody hot,' Napier grumbled at his side. 'I'm going to buy a parasol for walking about outdoors.'

Garamond was in no mood to respond to small talk. 'It's getting too much like Earth and Terranova.'

'You won't be able to prove the call was blocked.'

'I'm not even going to try.'

They walked quickly along the brown dirt road which threaded through the scattering of residences and reached the belt of small administrative buildings, research laboratories and windowless storehouses which surrounded the aperture. The black ellipse began to be disjointedly visible through a clutter of docking machinery and L-shaped entry ports. Garamond was no longer able to think of it as a lake of stars – now it was simply a hole in the ground. As they were passing an unusually large anonymous building his attention was caught by sunlight glinting on a moving vehicle – one of the few yet to be seen on Orbitsville. It stopped at the entrance to the building, four men got out and hurried inside. One of them had a youthful build which contrasted with his greying hair.

Napier caught Garamond's arm. 'That looked like our man.'

'We'll see.' They sprinted across a patch of grass and into the dense shade of the foyer, just in time to see an interior door closing. A doorman wearing Starflight emblems came out of a kiosk and tried to bar their way, but Garamond and Napier went by on each side of him and burst through to the inner room. Garamond's first glance confirmed that he had found Colbert Mason. The reporter was between two men who were gripping his arms, and three others – one of whom Garamond identified as Silvio Laker, a member of Elizabeth Lindstrom's personal staff – were standing close by. Mason's face had a dazed, drugged expression.

'Hands off him,' Garamond commanded.

'Out of here,' Laker said. 'You're outside your territory, Captain.'

'I'm taking Mason with me.'

'Like hell you are,' said one of the men holding Mason, stepping forward confidently.

Garamond gave him a bored look. 'I can cripple you ten different ways.' He was lying, never having been interested in even the recreational forms of personal combat, but the man suddenly looked less confident. While he was hesitating, his partner released Mason and tried to snatch something from his pocket, but was dissuaded by Napier who simply moved his three-hundred-pound bulk in a little closer and looked expectant. A ringing silence descended on the sparsely furnished room.

'Are you all right?' Garamond said to Mason.

'My neck,' the reporter said uncertainly, fingering a pink blotch just above his collar. 'They used a hypodermic spray on me.'

'It was probably just a sedative to keep you quiet.' Garamond fixed his gaze on Laker. 'For your sake, I hope that's right.'

'I warned you to stay out of this,' Laker said in a hoarse voice, his short round body quivering with anger. He extended his right fist, on which was a large gold ring set with a ruby.

'Lasers are messy,' Garamond said.

'I don't mind cleaning up.'

'You're getting in over your head, Laker. Have you thought about what Elizabeth would do to you for involving her in my murder?'

'I've an idea she'd like to see you put away.'

'In secret, yes – but not like this.' Garamond nodded to Napier. 'Let's go.' They turned the compliant, stupefied reporter around and walked him towards the door.

'I warn you, Garamond,' Laker whispered. 'I'm prepared to take the chance.'

'Don't be foolish.' Garamond spoke without looking back. The door was only a few paces away now and he could feel an intense tingling between his shoulder blades. He put out his hand to grasp the handle, but in the instant of his touching it the door was flung open and three more men exploded into the room. Garamond tensed to withstand an onslaught but the newcomers, two of whom were wearing field technician uniforms, brushed past with unseeing eyes.

'Mr Laker,' shouted the third man, who was wearing the blue uniform of a Starflight engineering officer. 'You've got to hear this! You'll never...'

Laker's voice was ragged with fury. 'Get out, Gordino. What the hell's the idea of bursting in here like . . . ?'

'But you don't understand! We've made contact with outsiders! Two of my technicians went over the hills to the west of here last night and they found an alien community – one that's still in use!'

Laker's jaw and threatening fist sagged in unison. 'What are you saying, Gordino? What kind of a story is this?'

'These are the two men, Mr Laker. They'll tell you about it themselves.'

'Two of your drunken gypsies.'

'Please.' The taller of the technicians raised his hand and spoke in an incongruous and strangely dignified voice. 'I anticipated a certain degree of scepticism, so instead of returning to base immediately I waited till daylight and took a number of photographs. Here they are.' He produced a sheaf of coloured rectangles and offered them to Laker. Garamond pushed Napier and the still-dazed Mason out through the door and, forgetting all notion of fleeing, strode back to Laker and snatched the photographs. Other hands were going for them as well, but he emerged from the free-for-all with two pictures. The background in each was the limitless prairie of Orbitsville and ranged across the middle distance were pale blue rectangles which could be nothing other than artificial structures. Near the base of some of the buildings were multicoloured specks, so small as to be represented only by pinpricks of pigment beneath the glaze of the photographs.

'These coloured dots,' Garamond said to the tall technician. 'Are they . . . ?'

'All I can say is that they moved. From the distance they look like flowers, but they move around.'

Garamond returned his attention to the pictures, trying to drive his mind down a converging beam at the focus of which were the bright-hued molecules – as if he could reach an atomic level where alien forms would become visible, and beyond it a nuclear level on which he could look into the faces and eyes of the first companions Man had found in all his years of star-searching. The reaction was a natural one, conditioned by centuries during which the sole prospect of contacting others lay in close examination of marks on photographic plates, but it was swept aside almost at once by forces of instinct. Garamond found himself walking towards the door and was out in the sunlight before understanding that he was heading for the Starflight vehicle parked near the entrance. The figures of Napier and Mason were visible a short distance along the road, apparently on their way to Garamond's house. He got into the crimson vehicle and examined the controls. The car was brand-new, having been manufactured on board one of the spaceships specifically for use on Orbitsville, and no keys were needed to energize the pulse-magnet engine. Garamond pressed the starter button and accelerated away in a cloud of dust as Laker and the others were coming out of the building.

He ignored their shouts, gunned the engine for the few seconds it took to catch up on Napier, brought his heel down on the single control pedal and skidded the car to a halt. He threw open a door. Napier glanced back at the Starflight men who were now in pursuit and, without needing to be told, bundled Mason into the vehicle and climbed in after him. The engine gave a barely perceptible whine as Garamond switched from heel to toe pressure on the pedal, sending the car snaking along the packed earth of the road as the excess of power forced its drive wheels to slide from side to side.

In less than a minute they had cleared the perimeter of the township and were speeding towards the sunlit hills.

*

The alien settlement came in view as soon as the car reached the crest of the circular range of hills. It was composed of pale blue rectangles shining in the distance like chips of ceramic. His brief study of the photographs had given Garamond the impression that the buildings were in a single cluster, but in actuality they spanned the entire field of view and extended out across the plain for several kilometres. Garamond realized he was looking at a substantial city. It was a city which appeared to lack a definite centre – but nevertheless large enough to sustain a population of a million or more, judging by human standards. Garamond eased back on the throttle, slowing the car's descent. He had just picked out the colourful moving specks which he believed were the first contemporaries mankind had ever encountered beyond the biosphere of his birth planet.

'Cliff, didn't I hear something about the Starflight science teams duplicating our experiment with a reconnaissance torpedo?' Garamond frowned as he spoke, his eyes fixed on the glittering city.

'I think so.'

'I wonder if the cameras were activated?'

'I doubt it. They could hardly have missed seeing this.'

Mason, who had recovered from his shot of sedative, stirred excitedly in the rear seat, panning with his scene recorder. 'What are you going to say to these beings, Captain?'

'It doesn't matter what any of us say – they won't understand it.'

'They mightn't even hear it,' Napier said. 'Maybe they don't have ears.'

Garamond felt his mouth go dry. He had visualized this moment many times, with a strength of yearning which could not be comprehended by anyone who had not looked into the blind orbs of a thousand lifeless worlds, but the prospect of coming face to face with a totally alien life form was upsetting his body chemistry. His heart began a slow, powerful pounding as the pale blue city rose higher beyond the nose of the car. Without conscious bidding, his foot eased further back on the throttle and the hum of the engine became completely inaudible at the lower speed. For a long moment there was no sound but that of the tough grasses of Orbitsville whipping at the vehicle's bodywork.

'What's the trouble, Vance?' Napier's eyes were watchful and sympathetic. 'Arachnid reaction?'

'I guess so.'

'Don't worry – I can feel it too.'

'Arachnid reaction?' Mason leaned forward eagerly. 'What's that?'

94

'Ask us some other time.'

'No, it's all right,' Garamond said, glad of the opportunity to talk. 'Do you like spiders?'

'I can't stand them,' Mason replied.

'That's fairly universal. The revulsion that most people get when they see spiders – arachnids – is so strong and widespread it has led to the theory that arachnids are not native to Earth. We have a sense of kinship, no matter how slight, with all creatures which originated on our own world, and this makes them acceptable to us even when they're as ugly as sin. But if the arachnid reaction is what some people think it is – loathing for something instinctively identified as of extraterrestrial origin – then we might be in trouble when we make the first contact with an alien race.

'The worry is that they might be intelligent and friendly, even beautiful, and yet might trigger off hate-and-kill reactions in us simply because their shape isn't already registered in a kind of checklist we inherit with our genes.'

'It's just an idea, of course.'

'Just an idea,' Garamond agreed.

'What's the probability of it being right?'

'Virtually zero, in my estimation. I wouldn't . . .' Garamond stopped speaking as the car lifted over a slight rise and he saw two bright-hued beings only a few hundred paces ahead. The aliens were a long way out from the perimeter of their city, isolated. He brought the car to a gradual halt.

'I guess . . . I have a feeling we ought to get out and walk the rest of the way.'

Napier nodded and swung open his door. They got out, paused for a moment in the heat of Orbitsville's constant noon, and began walking towards the two man-sized but unearthly figures. Mason followed with his scene recorder.

As the distance between them narrowed, Garamond began to discern the shape of the aliens and was relieved to discover he was not afraid of them in spite of the fact that they were un-like anything he had ever imagined. The creatures seemed, at first, to be humanoids wrapped in garments which were covered with large patches of pink, yellow and brown. At closer range, however, the garments proved to be varicoloured fronds which partly concealed complex, asymmetrical bodies. The aliens did not have clearly defined heads – merely regions of greater complexity at the tops of their blunt, forward-leaning trunks. From a wealth of tendrils, cavities and protuberances, the only organs Garamond was able to identify with any certainty were the eyes, which resembled twin cabochons of green bloodstone.

'What are they like?' Napier whispered.

'I don't know.' Garamond felt a similar need to relate the aliens to something from his past experience. 'Painted shrimps?'

He became aware that the reporter had fallen behind, and that he and Napier were now only a few paces from the aliens. Both men stopped walking and stood facing the fantastic creatures, which had not moved nor given any indication of being aware of their approach. Silence descended over the tableau like liquid glass, solidifying around them. The plain became a sun-filled lens and they were at the centre of it, immobilized and voiceless. Psychic pressures built up and became intolerable, and yet there was nothing to do or say.

Garamond's mind escaped into irrelevancy. *It doesn't matter that I wasn't able to think of anything to say for the benefit of posterity – there's no way to communicate. No way.*

A minute endured like an age, and then another.

'We've done our bit,' Napier announced finally. 'Let's go, Vance.'

Garamond turned thankfully and they walked towards Mason, who backed away from them, still holorecording all that was happening. Not until he had reached the car did Garamond look in the direction of the aliens. One of them was moving away towards its city with a complicated ungainly gait; the other was standing exactly where they had left it.

'I'll drive back,' Napier said, climbing into the car first and experimenting with the simplified controls while the others were taking their seats. He got the vehicle moving, swung it round and set off up the hill at an oblique angle. 'We'll go the long way round in case we run into a crowd following our tracks out.'

Garamond nodded, his thoughts still wholly absorbed by the two creatures on the plain. 'There was no arachnid reaction – I suppose that's something we can feel good about – but I felt totally inadequate. There was no point to it at all. I can't see us and them ever relating or interacting.'

'I don't know about relating, Vance, but there's going to be plenty of interacting.' Napier pointed out through the windshield to the left, where the curve of the hill was falling away to reveal new expanses of prairie. The pale blue buildings of the alien city, instead of thinning out, were spread across the fresh vistas of grassland like flowers in a meadow, seemingly going on for ever.

Mason whistled and raised his recorder. 'Do you think it makes a circle outside the hills ? Right round our base ?'

'It looks that way to me. They must have been here a long time . . .' Napier allowed his words to tail off, but Garamond knew at once what he was thinking.

Liz Lindstrom had brought a third of a million settlers with her on the very first load, and the big ships would soon be bringing land-hungry humans in batches of a full million or more. Interaction between the two races was bound to take place in the near future, and on a very large scale.

eleven

Rumours of massacre came within a month.

There had been a short-term lull while the shallow circular basin centred on Beachhead City absorbed the first waves of settlers. During this brief respite a handful of External Affairs representatives arrived, aware of their inadequacy, and ruled that no humans were to go within five kilometres of the alien community until negotiations had been completed for a corridor through to the free territory beyond. A number of factors combined against their efficacy, however. The Government men had been late on the scene, no broadcasting media were available to them, and – most important – there was a widespread feeling among the settlers that attempting diplomatic communication with the Clowns, as they had been unofficially named, would be an exercise in futility.

At first the bright-hued aliens had been approached with caution and respect, then it was learned that they possessed no machines beyond the simplest farming implements. Even their houses were woven from a kind of cellulose rope extruded from their own bodies in roughly the same way that a spider produces its web. When it was further discovered that the Clowns were mute, the assumption of their intelligence was called into question by many of the human settlers. One theory advanced was that they were degenerate descendants of the race which had built the fortifications around the Beachhead City aperture; another that they were little more than domestic animals which had outlived their masters and developed a quasiculture of their own.

Garamond was disturbed by the attitude implicit in the theories, partly because it was a catalyst for certain changes which were taking place in the Earth settlers. The subtle loosening of discipline he had noticed among his own men within minutes of their setting foot on Orbitsville had its counterpart among the immigrants in the form of a growing disregard for authority. Men whose lives had been closely controlled in the tight, compacted society of Earth now regarded themselves as potential owners of continents and were impatient for their new status. All they had to do to transform themselves from clerks to kings was to load up the vehicles provided by the Starflight workshops and set out on their golden journeys. The only directive was that they should travel far, because it was obvious that the further a man went when fanning out from Beachhead City the more land would be available to him.

As the mood took hold of the settlers even the earliest arrivals, who had staked out their plots of land within the circular hills, became uneasily aware of the incoming hordes at their heels and decided to move onwards and outwards.

In a normal planetary situation the population pressures would not have been concentrated so fiercely on one point, but Earth technology was geared to the Assumption of Mediocrity. During the development of the total transport system of flicker-wing ships and shuttles it had never occurred to anyone to make provision for an environment in which, for example, it would not be possible for a ship to gather its own reaction mass. It would have been completely illogical to do so, in the universe as it was then understood – but in the context of Orbitsville a deadly mistake had been made.

Territories of astronomical dimensions were available, but no means of claiming them quickly enough to satisfy the ambitions of men who had crossed space like gods and then found themselves reduced to wheeled transportation. Given time to build or import fleets of wing-borne aircraft, the difficulties could have been lessened but not removed completely. Each family unit or commune had to become self-supporting in the shortest possible time and, even with advanced farming methods and the use of iron cows, this meant claiming possession of large areas without delay.

It was a situation which, classically, had always resulted in man fighting man. Garamond was not surprised therefore when reports began to reach him that the outermost settlers had forced their way through the Clown city in a number of places and were pouring into the prairie beyond. He did not try to visit any of the trouble spots in person, but had no difficulty in visualizing the course of events at each. Still haunted by the sense of having lost his purpose, he devoted most of his time to his family, making only occasional visits to the *Bissendorf* in his capacity of chief executive. He deliberately avoided watching the newscasts which were piped into his home along the landlines, but other channels were open.

One morning, while he was sleeping off the effects of a prolonged drinking session, he was awakened by the sound of a child's scream. The sound triggered off a synergistic vision of Harald Lindstrom falling away from the blind face of a statue and, almost in the same instant, came the crushing awareness that he had not been sufficiently on his guard against Elizabeth.

Garamond sat up in bed, gasping for air, and lurched to the living-room. Aileen had got there before him and was kneeling with her arms around Christopher. The boy was now sobbing gently, his face buried in her shoulder.

'What happened?' Garamond's fear was subsiding but his heart was pounding unevenly.

'It was the projector,' Aileen said. 'One of those *things* appeared on it. I turned it off.'

'What things?' Garamond glanced at the projection area of the solid-image television where the faint ghost of a tutor in one of the educational programmes was still dissolving into the air.

Christopher raised a streaked, solemn face. 'It was a Crown.'

'He means a Clown.' Aileen's eyes were slaty with anger.

'A Clown? But ... I told you to keep the images fairly diffuse when Chris is watching so that he won't get confused between what's real and what isn't.'

'The image was diffused. The thing still scared him, that's all.'

Garamond stared helplessly at his wife. 'I don't get it. Why should he be afraid of a Clown?' He turned his attention to Christopher. 'What's the matter, son? Why were you afraid?'

'I thought the Crown was coming to get me too.'

'That was a silly thing to think – they never harmed anybody.'

The boy's gaze was steady and reproachful. 'What about all the people they froze? All the dead people?'

Garamond was taken aback. 'What do you mean?'

'Don't confuse him,' Aileen said quietly. 'You know perfectly well what's been in the newscasts for the last couple of days.'

'But I *don't*! What did they say?'

'About the outer planet. When they built Lindstromland they shut off all the light and heat to the outer planet and froze it over.'

'They? Who were they?'

'The Clowns, of course.'

'But that's wonderful!' Garamond began to smile. 'The Clowns created Orbitsville!'

'Their ancestors.'

'I see. And there were people on the outer planet? People who got frozen to death?'

'They showed photographs of them.' A stubborn note had crept into Aileen's voice.

'Where did they get these photographs?'

'A Starflight ship must have gone there, of course.'

'But, honey, if the planet is frozen over how could anybody take photographs of its surface or anything on it? Just try thinking it over for a while.'

'I don't know how they did it – I'm only telling you what Chris and I and everybody else have seen.'

Garamond sighed and walked to the communicator and called Cliff Napier on board the *Bissendorf*. The familiar head appeared almost immediately at the projection focus and nodded a greeting.

'Cliff, I need some information about ship movements within the Pengelly's Star system.' Garamond spoke quickly, without preamble. 'Has there been an expedition to the outer planet?'

'No.'

'You're positive?'

Napier glanced downwards, looking at an information display. 'Absolutely.'

'Thanks, Cliff. That's all.' Garamond broke the connection and Napier's apparently solid features faded into the air just as an expression of puzzlement was appearing on them. 'There you are, Aileen – a direct, clear statement of fact. Now, where are the photographs supposed to have come from?'

'Well, perhaps they weren't actual photographs. They might have been . . .'

'Artists' impressions? Reconstructions?'

'What difference does it make? They were shown . . .'

'*What difference?*' Garamond gave a shaky laugh as the mental chasm opened between himself and his wife, but he felt no annoyance with her. Their marriage had always been simple and harmonious, and he knew it was based on deeper attachments than could be achieved through mere similarity in interests or outlook. One of the first things he had learned to accept was the certainty of lasting incompleteness on some levels of their relationship, and usually he knew how to accommodate it.

'It makes all the difference in the world,' he said softly, almost as if speaking to a child. 'Don't you see how your attitude towards the Clowns has been affected by what you've seen or think you've seen on the viewers ? That's the way people are manipulated. It used to be more difficult, or at least they had to be more subtle when literacy was considered vital to education . . .' Even to his own ears the words sounded dry and irrelevant, and he stopped speaking as he noticed Aileen's predictable loss of interest. His wife absorbed most of her information semi-instinctively, through images, and he had no picture to show her. Garamond felt an obscure sadness.

'I'm not stupid, Vance.' Aileen touched his hand, her intuition in sure control.

'I know.'

'What did you want to tell me ?'

'I just want you to remember the Starflight Corporation is like . . .' he strove for a suitably vivid image, '. . . like a snowball rolling down a hill. It keeps getting bigger and bigger, and it keeps going faster, and it can't slow down. It can't afford to stop, even when somebody gets in the way . . . and that's why it's going to roll right on over the Clowns.'

'You always seem so certain about things.'

'The signs are all there. The first step is to implant in people's minds the idea that the Clowns *ought* to be rolled over. Once that's been done the rest is easy.'

'I don't like the Crowns,' Christopher said, breaking a long silence. His grain-gold face was determined.

'I'm not asking you to like them, son. Just don't believe that everything you see on the viewer is real and true. Why, if I went to the outer planet myself I could . . .' Garamond stopped speaking for a moment as the idea took hold of his mind.

*

'Why not ? After all, that's the sort of work the S.E.A. ships were designed to do,' Elizabeth had said, reasonably, and at that point she had smiled. 'You're on indefinite leave, Captain, but if you would prefer to return to active service and visit the outer world I have no objections.'

'Thank you, My Lady,' Garamond had replied, concealing his surprise.

Elizabeth's imperfect smile had grown more secretive, more triumphant. 'We will find it very useful to possess some hard data about the planet – in place of all the speculations which are filling the air.'

*

Garamond reviewed the brief conversation many times during the period in which the *Bissendorf* was extending its invisible wings and disengaging from fleet formation. It came to him that he had proposed the exploratory flight partly as a challenge to the President, hoping that a duel with her would ease the growing tensions in his mind. Her ready agreement to the mission was the last thing he had expected and, as well as drawing a few pointed comments from Aileen, it had left him feeling both disappointed and uneasy.

He sat in the control gallery for hours, watching the bright images of the other Starflight ships perform the patient manoeuvres which would bring each one in turn to the entrance of Orbitsville where it could discharge its load of human beings or supplies. When the *Bissendorf*'s own progression had taken it out through the regulated swarm, and nothing but stars lay in front, Garamond remained on station watching the irregular stabs of the main electron gun, the ghostly blade of energy which flickered through space ahead of the ship. The harvest of reaction mass was not plentiful in the immediate vicinity of Pengelly's Star and in the early stages of the flight it was necessary to ionize the cosmic dust to help the intake fields do their work. Gradually, however, as the ship spiralled outwards, the night-black plain of Orbitsville's shell ceased to blank off an entire half of the visible universe. The conditions of space became more normal and speed began to build up. Once again Garamond had difficulty in setting his perceptions to the correct scale. Everything in his past experience conspired to make him think he was in a tiny ship which was painfully struggling to a height of a few hundred kilometres above a normal-sized planet, whereas at a hundred million kilometres out it was still necessary to turn one's head through ninety degrees to take in both edges of Orbitsville's disc.

The size of the sphere was, in a way, painful to Garamond, causing familiar questions to seethe again in his mind. Was the fact that it was large enough to accommodate every intelligent being in the home galaxy a clue to its purpose? Why was there only one entrance to such a huge edifice? Did the physics of the sphere's existence dictate of necessity that neither flicker-wing ship nor radio communicator could operate inside it? Or were those features designed in by the Creators to preserve the sphere's effective size, and to prevent ingenious technicians turning it into a global village with their FTL ships and television networks? And where were the Creators now?

Napier appeared with two bulbs of coffee, one of which he handed to Garamond. 'The weather section reports that the local average density of space is increasing according to their predictions. That means we should be able to pick up enough speed to reach the outer planet in not much more than a hundred hours.'

Garamond nodded his approval. 'The probe torpedo should be fitted out by then.'

'Sammy Yamoto wants to lead a manned descent to the surface.'

'That could be dangerous – we'll have to get a better report on the surface conditions before authorizing anything like that.' Garamond began to sip his coffee, then frowned. 'Why should our Chief Astronomer want to risk his neck out there? I thought he was still wrapped up in his globular filigree of force fields.'

'He is, but he reckons he can deduce a few things about how Orbitsville was built by examining the outer planet.'

'Tell him to keep me posted.' Garamond looked at Napier over the mouthpiece of his coffee bulb and saw an uncharacteristic look of hesitancy on the big man's face. 'Anything else coming to the boil?'

'Shrapnel seems to have gone AWOL.'

'Shrapnel? The shuttle pilot?'

'That's right.'

'So he took off. Isn't that what we expected?'

'I expected him to do it once, but not twice. He disappeared for the best part of a day soon after the Starflight crowd got here. It was during the time he was on ground detachment so I decided he had gone back to Starflight with a hard luck story, and I wrote him off – but he was back on duty again that night.'

'That surprised you?'

'It did, especially as he came back without the chip on his shoulder. His whole attitude seemed to have changed for the better, and since then he's been working like a beaver.'

'Maybe he discovered he didn't like the Starflight HQ staff.'

Napier looked unconvinced. 'He didn't object or try to cry off when orders were posted for this flight, but he isn't on board.'

'I'd just forget about him.'

'I'm trying to,' Napier said, 'but the *Bissendorf* isn't a sailing ship tied up in a harbour. A man who is able to come and go unofficially must have some organization behind him. It makes me think Shrapnel had contacts in Starflight.'

'Let's have some whisky,' Garamond suggested. 'We're both getting too old for this type of work.'

*

Even before it was denied the light and heat of its own sun, the outer planet of the Pengelly's Star system had been a bleak, sterile place.

Less than half the size of Earth, and completely devoid of atmosphere, it was a ball of rock and dust which patrolled a lonely orbit so far out that its parent sun appeared as little more than a bright star casting barely perceptible shadows in an inert landscape. And when that sun vanished it made very little difference to the planet. Its surface became a little colder and a little darker, but the cooling stresses were not great enough to cause anything as spectacular as movements of the crust. Nothing stirred in the blackness, except for infrequent puffs of dust from meteor strikes, and the uneventful millennia continued to drag by as they had always done.

*

Using its radar fans like the feelers of a giant insect, the *Bissendorf* groped its way into orbit around the invisible sphere which was the dead world.

The ship was in the form of three equal cylinders joined together, with the central one projecting forward from the other two by almost half its length. The command deck, administrative and technical levels, living quarters and workshops were contained in the central cylinder. This exposed position meant the inhabited regions of the vessel could have been subjected to an intense bombardment during high speed flight, when – due to the ship's own velocity – even stationary motes of interstellar dust registered as fantastically energetic particles. The problem had been solved by using the same magnetic deflection techniques which guided the particles into the ramjet's thermonuclear reactors. Both the *Bissendorf*'s flux pumps shaped their magnetic lines of force into the form of a protective shield around which the charged particles flowed harmlessly into the engines.

An inherent disadvantage of the system was that a starship could never coast at high speed – with the flux pumps closed down the crew would quickly have been fried in self-induced radiation. Communications with a ship which was under way were also precluded, and under these conditions even radar sensing could not be employed. The approach to the dark planet had been made at modest interplanetary speeds, however, and the *Bissendorf* was able to proceed by using its main drive in short bursts, between which it was possible to run position checks. Because it was designed for exploration work in unknown planetary systems, the vessel was further equipped with conventional nuclear thrusters and a limited amount of stored reaction mass which gave it extra capability for close manoeuvring. The task of slipping into stable orbit was therefore accomplished quickly and efficiently, even though the target planet remained invisible to the *Bissendorf*'s crew.

It took only one pass to enable the long-range sensors and recording banks to answer all of Garamond's questions.

'This is pretty disappointing,' Sammy Yamoto said as he examined the glowing numerals and symbols of the preliminary analysis. 'The planet has no atmosphere now and appears never to have had one at any time in its past. Its surface is completely barren. I was hoping for the remains of some kind of plant life which would have told us whether the radiation from the primary was cut off suddenly or over a period of years.'

Chief Science Officer O'Hagan said, 'We can still do a lot with samples of dust and rock from the surface.'

Yamoto nodded without enthusiasm. 'I guess so, but botanical evidence would have been so precise. So *nice*. With nothing but inorganic evidence we're going to have margins of error of what? A thousand years or more?'

'On an astronomical timescale that's not bad.'

'It's not bad, but it's not . . .'

'Is it the opinion of the group,' Garamond put in, 'that a manned descent is still worth while?'

O'Hagan glanced around the other science officers who were anchored close to the information display, then shook his head. 'At this stage it would be enough to drop a robolander and take three or four cores. Somebody can always come back if the cores prove to be of exceptional interest, but I don't hold out much hope.'

'Right – it's decided we send down one probe.' Garamond used his end-of-meeting voice. 'Get it down there and back again as quickly as possible, and include flares and holorecording gear in the package – I want to be able to present certain people with visible evidence.'

Denise Serra, the physicist, raised her eyebrows. 'I heard the Starflight Information Bureau was propagating some fantasy about a beautiful civilization being snuffed out in its prime, but I didn't believe it. I mean, who would swallow an idea like that?'

'You'd be surprised,' Garamond told her ruefully. 'I've been learning that there are different kinds of naïvety. We're subject to one kind – it's an occupational hazard associated with spending half your life cut off from the big scene – but there are others just as dangerous.'

'That may be so, but to believe that the Clowns created Orbitsville!'

'Genuine belief isn't required – the story is only a formula which allows certain manipulations to be carried out. We all know the square root of minus one is an unreal quantity, and yet we've all used it when it suited us to do so. Same thing.'

Denise's eyes twinkled. 'It isn't the same.'

'I know, but my statement was an example of the general class of thing we were talking about.'

'Neat footwork.' Denise laughed outright and, for no reason which was immediately apparent to him, Garamond suddenly became aware of how much he enjoyed simply looking at her. He had accepted the phrase 'easy on the eyes' as pure metaphor but now was surprised to discover that letting his gaze rest on the physicist's pale sensitive face actually produced a soothing sensation in his eyes. The phenomenon entranced and then disturbed him.

When the meeting broke up he went to his own quarters and devoted several hours to his principal spare-time occupation of recording television interviews for Colbert Mason. The reporter, after his initial difficulties on Orbitsville, had established himself in a position of relative strength, and had obtained an office in Beachhead City from which he sent back a prolific stream of news stories for syndication on the Two Worlds. Garamond co-operated with him as much as he could, mainly because in his estimation his personal fame was still his family's best protection against Elizabeth Lindstrom.

There were times when he was almost persuaded by Aileen that he was wrong in his suspicions of the President, but against that there were persistent rumours that she had slain a member of her domestic staff who had found her son's body. Garamond continued to maintain his defences. The system was that Mason supplied him with tridi tapes of recorded questions and when it was convenient Garamond used his own equipment to fill in his answers and comments. On a number of occasions Mason had confessed that he was making a fortune from the arrangement and had proposed sharing the profits but Garamond had refused to accept any money, stipulating only that Mason obtain for him the widest possible exposure. It appeared that this objective was being achieved because there was a growing clamour for the discoverer of Lindstromland to make a personal return to Earth.

Garamond spent most of the current session giving suitable reasons for not being able to return and in describing, in precise details, what had been learned about the invisible planet. Assuming the material would be safely relayed to the Two Worlds by Mason and broadcast on the planet-wide networks, he had gone a long way towards killing any suggestion that the Clowns or any other beings connected with Orbitsville had obliterated an entire civilization.

He stored the tapes away carefully, again wondering at the great latitude Elizabeth was permitting him, and fastened himself into his bed with the intention of catching up on his sleep. The slow-drifting cubes of coloured radiance merged and shimmered in the air above him, creating hypnotic patterns. Once more there came the idea that he might be completely wrong about Elizabeth Lindstrom, and he found himself wishing it were possible to discuss the subject emotionlessly and intellectually with his wife. There would be, he decided sleepily, no communications problem with a woman like Denise Serra who shared his background and his interests, and who produced the curiously pleasant sensation in his eyes when he . . .

Garamond slept.

He awoke two hours later with an unaccountable sense of unease and decided to put a call through to Aileen and Christopher before going out on to the control gallery. The communications room made the necessary connection and in less than a minute Garamond was looking at the image of his wife, but a winking sphere of amber told him he was viewing and hearing a recording. It said:

'I was hoping you would call, Vance. I know you are only making a short trip, but Chris and I have got so used to having you with us lately that we are spoiled and the time is passing very slowly. Something very exciting has happened, though. You'll never guess.' The unreal Aileen paused for a moment, smiling, to demonstrate to Garamond his inability to divine what was coming next.

'I had a personal call from the President – yes, Elizabeth

109

Lindstrom herself – inviting Chris and me to stay with her in the new Lindstrom Centre for a few days . . .'

'Don't go!' Garamond was unable to restrain the words.

'. . . knew I'd be feeling lonely while you were away,' the image was saying contentedly, 'but what really decided me was that she said she was the one who would benefit most from the visit. She didn't actually put it into words, but I think she is looking forward to seeing a child about the place again. Anyway, Vance, I must go now – the President's car is calling for us in a few minutes. By the time you hear this I'll be wallowing in luxury and high living at the Octagon, but don't worry – I'll be at home to cook you a meal when you arrive. Love you, darling. Bye.'

The image dissolved into a cloud of fading stars, leaving Garamond cold, shaken, and angry at his wife. 'You silly bitch,' he whispered to the fleeting points of light. 'Why do you never ever, *never ever*, listen to anything I tell you ?'

The last handful of stars vanished in silence.

*

The probe torpedo worked its way up the gravity hill from the dead planet, carrying its samples of dust and rock, and homed in on the *Bissendorf*. Although there was a sun only three astronomical units away, its light was screened off and the torpedo was moving through a blackness equivalent to that of deep interstellar space. In that darkness the mother ship appeared to some of the probe's sensors as a faint cluster of lights, but to other sensors concerned with different sections of the electromagnetic spectrum the ship registered as a brilliant beacon whose radiation embodied many voices commanding, guiding, coaxing it homewards. Responding with greater and greater precision as the electronic voices grew louder, the torpedo approached the ship with the familiarity of a parasite fish flittering about a whale. At last it made physical contact and was taken on board.

During the final manoeuvres Garamond had waited on the *Bissendorf*'s control gallery with growing impatience. As soon as the signal announcing closure of the docking bay was received he gave the order for the main drive to be activated. Initial impetus was given to the ship by the relatively feeble ion thrusters, but that propulsion system was shut down when the ramjet intake field had been fanned out to its maximum area of half a million square kilometres and reaction mass was being scavenged from the surrounding space. As the scooped-up hydrogen and other matter were fed into the fusion reactors the ship wheeled away sunwards, and the acceleration restored close-to-normal gravity throughout the inhabited levels of the central cylinder.

The feeling of the deck pressing firmly on the underside of his feet helped Garamond to regain his composure. He assured himself that if Elizabeth were to move against his family it would be done anywhere but in the crystal cloisters of her new residence. Into the bargain, Elizabeth knew that Garamond would be back from the dark planet in only a few days, imbued with an even greater amount – if that were possible – of the power called fame. The hours and the duty periods went by and, as Orbitsville filled the forward view panels with its unrelieved blackness, Garamond was able to satisfy himself that he had panicked for no good reason.

The *Bissendorf* had accomplished turnover at mid-point on the return journey, and was two days into the retardation phase, when explosions occurred simultaneously in both field generators, robbing the vessel of its means of coming to a halt before it would smash into the impregnable outer shell of Orbitsville.

twelve

'The starboard explosion was the worst,' Commander Napier reported to the emergency meeting of the *Bissendorf*'s executive staff. 'It actually breached the pressure hull in the vicinity of Frame S.203. The pressure-activated doors functioned properly and sealed off the section between Frames S.190 and 210, but there were five technicians in there at the time, and they were killed.'

O'Hagan raised his grey head. 'Blast or decompression?'

'We don't know – the bodies were exhausted into space.'

'I see.' O'Hagan made a note on his pad, speaking aloud at the same time. 'Five missing, presumed dead.'

Napier stared at his old antagonist with open dislike. 'If you know how we can turn the ship to recover the bodies this would be a good time to tell us about it.'

'I merely . . .'

'Gentlemen!' Garamond slapped the table as loudly as was possible in conditions of almost zero gravity. 'May I remind you that we are scheduled to be killed in about eight hours? That doesn't leave much time for bickering.'

O'Hagan gave a ghastly smile. 'It gives us eight hours for bickering, Captain – there's nothing else we can do.'

'That's for this meeting to decide.'

'So be it.' Chief Science Officer O'Hagan shrugged and spread his dry knobbly hands in resignation.

Garamond felt a reluctant admiration for the older man who seemed determined to remain egotistical and cantankerous right to the end. O'Hagan also had a habit of being right in everything he said, and in that respect too it seemed he was going to preserve his record. Although reaction mass was not plentiful in the region of Pengelly's Star, the *Bissendorf* had been aided in its return journey by the pull of the primary and had achieved a mean acceleration of close on one gravity. Modest though the acceleration and distances were, the ship had been travelling at 1,500 kilometres a second at turn-over point and, although it had been slowing down steadily for two days when the explosions occurred, its residual velocity was still above a hundred kilometres in each second. At that speed it was due to impact with Orbitsville in only eight hours, and it appeared to Garamond that there was nothing he or anybody else on board could do about it. The knowledge boomed and pounded beneath all other thoughts, and yet he felt a surprising absence of fear or any related emotion. It was, he decided, a psychological by-product of having eight hours in hand. The delay created the illusion that something might still be done, that there was a chance to influence the course of events in their favour, and – miraculously – this held good even for an experienced flicker-wing man who understood only too well the deadly parameters of his situation.

'I understand that both auxiliary drive systems are still functional,' Administrative Officer Mertz was saying, his round face glowing like pink plastic. 'Surely that makes a difference.'

Napier shook his head. 'The ion tubes are in action right now – which accounts for the very slight weight you can feel – but they were intended only to give the ship a close-manoeuvring capability, and they won't affect our speed very much. I guess the only difference they'll make is that we'll vaporize against Orbitsville a minute or two later than we would otherwise.'

'Well, how about the secondary nuclears? I thought they were for collision avoidance.'

'They are. Maximum endurance twenty minutes. By applying full thrust at right angles to our present course we could easily avoid an object as large as Jupiter – but we're dealing with *that*.' Napier pointed at the forward view panels, which were uniformly black. Orbitsville was spanning the universe.

'I see.' Mertz's face lost some of its pinkness. 'Thank you.'

The operations room filled with a silence which was broken only by faint irregular clangs transmitted through the ship's structure. Far aft, a repair crew was at work replacing the damaged hull sections. Garamond stared into the darkness ahead and tried to assimilate the idea that it represented a wall across the sky, a wall which was rushing towards him at a hundred kilometres a second, a wall so wide and high that there was no way to avoid hitting it.

Yamoto cleared his throat. 'There's no point in speculating about why the ship was sabotaged, but do we know how the bombs got on board?'

'I personally believe it was done by Pilot Officer Shrapnel,' Napier said. 'There isn't much evidence, but what there is points to him. We gave all the information in our emergency call to Fleet Control.'

'What did they say?'

'They promised he would be investigated.' Napier's voice had a flinty edge of bitterness. 'We are assured that all necessary steps will be taken.'

'That's good to know. Isn't that good to know?' Yamoto pressed the back of a hand to his forehead. 'I had so much work still to do. There was so much to learn about Orbitsville.'

They're going to learn at least one thing as a result of this mission, Garamond thought. *They're going to find out how the shell material stands up to the impact of fifteen thousand tons of metal travelling at a hundred kilometres a second. And they won't even have to go far from the aperture to see the big bang . . .* Garamond felt an icy convulsion in his stomach as he half-glimpsed an idea. He sat perfectly still for a moment as the incredible thought began to form, to crystallize to the point at which it could be put into words. His brow grew chill with sweat.

'Has anybody,' Denise Serra asked in a calm, clear voice, 'considered the possibility of adjusting our course in such a way that we would pass through the aperture at Beachhead City?'

Again the room filled with silence. Garamond felt a curious secondary shock on hearing the words he was still formulating being uttered by another person. The silence lasted for perhaps ten seconds, then was broken by a dry laugh from O'Hagan.

'You realize that, at our speed, running into a wall of air would be just like hitting solid rock? I'm afraid your idea doesn't change anything.'

'We don't have to run into a wall of air – not if we turn the ship over again and go in nose first with the electron gun operating at full power.'

'Nonsense,' O'Hagan shouted. He cocked his head to one side as if listening to an inner voice and his fingers moved briefly on the computer terminal before him. 'It isn't nonsense, though.' He corrected himself without embarrassment, nodding his apologies to Denise Serra, and others at the conference table began to address the central computer through their own terminals.

'Overload power on the gun should give us enough voltage for the few seconds we would need it. It should be enough to blast a tunnel through the atmosphere.'

'At this stage we have enough lateral control over our flight path to bring it through the aperture.'

'But remember we haven't got the full area of the aperture as a target. We'd be going in at an angle of about seventy degrees.'

'It's still good enough – as long as no other ships get in the way.'

'There's still time to do some structural strengthening on the longitudinal axis.'

'We'll shed enough kinetic energy . . .'

'Hold it a minute,' Garamond commanded, raising his voice above the suddenly optimistic clamour, 'We have to look at it from all angles. If we did go through the aperture, what would be the effect on Beachhead City?'

'Severe,' O'Hagan said reflectively. 'Imagine one purple hell of a lightning bolt coming up through the aperture immediately followed by an explosion equivalent to a tactical nuclear weapon.'

'There'd be destruction?'

'Undoubtedly. But there's plenty of time to evacuate the area – nobody would have to die.'

'Somebody mentioned colliding with another ship.'

'That's a minor problem, Vance.' O'Hagan looked momentarily surprised at having used Garamond's given name for the first time in his life. 'We can advise Fleet Control of our exact course and they'll just have to make certain the way is clear.'

Garamond tried to weigh the considerations, but he could see only the faces of his wife and child. 'Right! We do it. I want to see a copy of the decision network plan, but start taking action right away. In the meantime I'll talk to Fleet Control.'

The ten science-oriented and engineering officers at the table instantly launched into a polygonal discussion and the noise level in the room shot up as communications channels were opened to other parts of the ship. Within a minute perhaps thirty other men and women were taking part, many of them vicariously present in the form of miniaturized, but nonetheless

115

solid and real-looking, images of their heads, which transformed the long room into a montage of crazy perspectives.

Garamond could almost feel the wavecrest of hope surging through all the levels of the disabled vessel. He told Napier to make an announcement about the situation on the general address system, then went into his private suite and put a call through to Fleet Control. It was taken not by the Fleet Movements Controller, as Garamond had expected, but by a Starflight admin man, Senior Secretary Lord Nettleton. The Senior Secretary was a handsome silver-haired man who had a reputation for his devotion to the Lindstrom hierarchy. He was of a type that Elizabeth liked to have around, capable of presenting a benign fatherly image, while keeping himself remote from the inner workings of the system.

'I was expecting somebody on the operations side,' Garamond said, dispensing with the standard formal mode of address.

'The President has taken the matter under her personal control. She is very much concerned.'

'I'll bet she is.'

'I beg your pardon?' Nettleton's resonant voice betrayed a degree of puzzlement which was an open challenge to Garamond to speak his mind.

Again Garamond thought about his wife and child. 'The President's concern for the welfare of her employees is well known.'

Nettleton inclined his head graciously. 'I'm aware of how futile words are under the circumstances, Captain Garamond, but I would like to express my personal sympathy for you and your crew in this . . .'

'The reason I called is to inform Starflight that the *Bissendorf* has enough lateral control to enable it to pass through the aperture into the interior of Orbits . . . Lindstromland, and that is what I intend to do.'

'I don't quite understand.' Nettleton's image underwent several minute but abrupt changes of size which told Garamond other viewers were switching into the circuit. 'I am informed that you are travelling at a hundred kilometres a second and have no means of slowing down.'

116

'That's correct. The *Bissendorf* is going to hit Beachhead City like a bomb. You will have to evacuate the area around the aperture. My science staff can help with the estimates of how widespread the damage will be, but in any case I strongly recommend that you issue warnings immediately. You have less than eight hours.' Garamond went on to explain the proposed action in detail, while continued perturbations of the image showed that his unseen audience was increasing every second.

'Captain, what happens if your ship misses the aperture and strikes the shell material below the city itself?'

'We are confident of passing through the aperture.'

'All you're saying is that the probability is high, but supposing you *do* miss?'

'It is our opinion that the shell would be undamaged.'

'But the shell is one of the greatest scientific enigmas ever known – on what do you base your predictions about its behaviour under that sort of impact?'

Garamond allowed himself a smile. 'In the last hour or so our instinct about these things has become highly developed.'

'This is hardly a time for jokes.' Nettleton looked away for a moment, nodded to someone off screen, and when he turned back to Garamond his eyes were sombre. 'Captain, have you thought about the possibility that Starflight may not be able to grant you permission to aim for the aperture?'

Garamond considered the question. 'No – but I've thought about the fact that there is absolutely nothing Starflight can do to stop me.'

Nettleton shook his head with regal sadness. 'Captain, I'm going to put you through to the President on a direct connection.'

'I haven't the time to speak to her,' Garamond told him. 'Just send a message to my wife that I'll be back with her as soon as I can.' He broke the connection and returned to the operations room, hoping he had sounded more confident than he felt.

*

Lindstrom Centre was austere compared to its equivalent on Earth, but it was the largest and most palatial building on Orbitsville. It was octagonal in plan and had been built on a slight eminence some twenty kilometres east from Beachhead City, to which it was joined by power and communication cables stretched on low pylons. No attempt had yet been made to sculpt the hill according to the President's ideas of what it ought to be, so the glass-and-acrylic edifice was incongruously lapped by a sea of grass. Its first three floors housed those elements of the Starflight administration which the supreme executive had transported from the Two Worlds, and the top floor was her private residence.

On this evening, the guards who patrolled the perimeter fence were distinctly uneasy. They had heard that a maniac of a flickerwing captain was going to try to crash his vessel through the aperture at interplanetary speed, and the rumour had even quoted an exact minute for the event to occur – 20.06 Compatible Local Time. As the moment grew nearer each man felt a powerful urge to fix his gaze on the distant scattering of buildings, just below the upcurved horizon, which was Beachhead City. They had been told that most of the city had been hastily evacuated to escape the promised pyrotechnics, and nobody wanted to miss the spectacle.

At the same time, however, their eyes were frequently drawn upwards to the transparent west wall of the Presidential suite. Elizabeth Lindstrom herself could be glimpsed up there, screened only by sky reflections, her silk-sheathed abdomen glowing like a pearl – and it was well known that she sometimes kept watch on her guards through a magnifying screen. None of the men relished the idea of being dismissed from Starflight service and sent back to the crowded towerblocks of Earth, and yet the compulsion to stare into the west grew greater with each passing minute.

The suspense was also making itself felt on the top floor of the Octagon, but in the case of Elizabeth Lindstrom it was a pleasurable sensation, heady and stimulating, akin to pre-orgasmic tension.

'My dear,' she said warmly to Aileen Garamond, 'do you think you are wise to watch this?'

'Quite sure, My Lady.'

'But the boy . . .'

'I'm positive my husband knows what he is doing.' Aileen's voice was firm and unemotional as she laid her hands on her son's shoulders, forcing him to face the west. 'Nothing will go wrong.'

'I admire your courage, especially when the chances are so...' Elizabeth checked herself just in time. The common, characterless woman beside her appeared genuinely to believe that a ship could run into a solid wall of air at a speed of a hundred kilometres a second and not be destroyed on the instant. Elizabeth was girded with the mathematics which showed how incredible the idea was, but she knew the equations would mean nothing to her guest. In any case, she had no desire to break the news in advance – she wanted to watch Mrs Garamond's face as she saw her husband's funeral pyre blossom on the horizon. Only then would she receive the first payment against the incalculable debt which the Garamond family owed her.

The concept of grief cancelling grief, of pain atoning for pain, was one which few people could properly understand, Elizabeth had often told herself. Even she had not appreciated the logic of it until days after Harald's small body had been cast in suncoloured resin and stood in its place in the Lindstrom chapel. But it was so *true*!

There were no flaws in the system of double entries – anguish against anguish, love against love – and this realization had given Elizabeth the strength to go on, even when it appeared that the Garamonds had chosen to die in the black deeps of space. That episode had been nothing more and nothing less than God's way of telling her that he was simply building up the Garamond's credit to the point at which it could be used to wipe out all their debts. In retrospect, it had been fortunate that she had not been able to extract payment immediately, because there would still have been an imbalance and she would never have found her heart's ease. A child is a focus, a repository of love which is added to in each year of its life, and it was crystal-clear that the death of a boy of nine could never be compensated for by the death of a boy of . . .

'I have the latest computations for you, My Lady.' The projected voice of Lord Nettleton broke in on Elizabeth's thoughts. 'The impact will occur in exactly three minutes from . . . now.'

'Three minutes,' Elizabeth said aloud, knowing that the accurately beamed sound would not have reached the other woman's ears. Without giving any sign that she had heard, Aileen picked her son up and her face was screened by the boy's body. Elizabeth moved quietly to the other side, as was her due, and waited.

She waited through eons and eternities.

And the ribbed canopy of the sky ceased to turn.

Time was dead . . .

The lightning bolt came first. An arrow-straight line of hell, searing upwards at an angle into the heavens, isolated for the first perceptible instant, then joined by writhing offshoots, tributaries and deltas of violet fire which flickered and froze on the retina. Faint shadows fled across the sky as the air above Beachhead City was hurled outwards by the fountain of energy. Appalling though the general display was, there existed at its core – on the threshold of vision – a sense of even greater forces in the shock of opposition. There was a feeling of cataclysmic upward movement, then a bright star burned briefly and dwindled in the south-west. The day returned to normalcy, but seemingly darker than it had been before.

Elizabeth drew a deep quavering breath – no other death she had ever witnessed had been so final. She turned her gaze on to Aileen Garamond's face, and was shocked to see there a look of serenity.

'It was to be expected,' she said.

'I know.' Aileen nodded contentedly, and hugged her child. 'I told you.'

Elizabeth gaped at her. 'You *fool*! You don't think he's still alive after what you've just . . .' She was forced to stop speaking as the waves of thunder rolling out from Beachhead City, slow moving in the low-pressure air of Orbitsville, engulfed the building. Reflections of lights stretched and shrank and stretched again as the transparent walls absorbed energy, and small objects throughout the room stirred uneasily in their places. Christopher buried his face in his mother's hair.

'Your husband is dead,' Elizabeth announced when silence was restored to the room. 'but because you are the widow of the most distinguished of all my S.E.A. captains, you will remain here as my guest. No other arrangement would be acceptable.'

Aileen faced her, pale but immovable. 'My Lady, you are mistaken. You see – I *know*.'

Elizabeth shook her head incredulously and a little sadly. She had been planning to spend perhaps a year in a game of subtleties and suggestions, watching the other woman's slow progression from doubt to certainty about her son's eventual fate. But it was obvious now – in view of Aileen Garamond's mentality, or lack of it – that such strategies would be ineffective. If the full payment were to be extracted, as God had decreed it should be, she would have to speak plainly, in words a child could understand. Elizabeth touched a beautiful micro-engineered ring on her left hand, ensuring that no listening devices could remain in operation nearby, and then explained the accountancy of retribution which demanded that Christopher Garamond should be allowed another three years. He was to have the same lifespan as Harald Lindstrom – but not a day longer.

When she had finished she summoned her physician. 'Captain Garamond's death has left Mrs. Garamond in a state of hysteria. Give her suitable sedation.'

Aileen opened her mouth to scream but the physician, an experienced man, touched her wrist in a quick movement which did not even disturb the boy she was holding in her arms. As the cloud of instant-acting drug sighed through her skin Aileen relaxed and allowed herself to be led away.

Alone again, Elizabeth Lindstrom stood looking out across the western grasslands and was aware – for the first time in over a year – of something approaching happiness. She began to smile.

thirteen

The integrity of the *Bissendorf*'s design was so great, and the onboard preparation had been so thorough, that less than a tenth of the crew died as a result of the passage through the eye of the needle.

Every available man and woman had been co-opted on to the teams which had welded into place a new computer-designed structure, creating load paths which actually utilized the forces of the impact to give the shell enough strength to survive. Until only a matter of minutes before the hellish transit, other gangs had swarmed on the outside of the ship, adding hundreds of sacrificial anodes to those which were already in place serving as focal points for the ion exchange which would otherwise have eaten away the hull during normal flight. The new anodes, massive slabs of pure metal, withstood the brief but incredibly fierce attrition of the lightning which wreathed the ship as it passed along the atmospheric tunnel created by its electron gun. On emerging from its ordeal the *Bissendorf*'s principal dimensions had altered, in some cases by several metres, but it had gone in with all pressure doors sealed – in effect it had been converted into dozens of separate, self-contained spaceships – and there was no loss of life due to decompression.

The entire crew had donned spacesuits for primary protection. Each person had been injected with metallic salts and the ship's restraint fields stepped up to overload intensity, creating an environment in which any sudden movement of human tissue would be resisted by a pervasive jelly-like pressure from all sides. This measure, while undoubtedly a major factor in crew survival, also caused an unavoidable number of deaths. In the few sections where severe structural failure occurred some of the occupants had 'fallen' varying distances under multiple gravities, and the heat induced by electromotive interaction had caused their blood to boil. But, for the vast majority, the internal bracing of their organs against immense G-shocks had meant the difference between life and death.

And yet, all the preparation, all the frenzied activity, would have amounted to nothing more than a temporary stay of execution had it not been for the exotic nature of Orbitsville itself.

The synthetic gravity of the shell material attenuated much more rapidly than that of a solid mass. Although the *Bissendorf*'s slanting course was drawn into the shape of a parabola the curve remained flat, and the crew had sufficient time to control their re-entry into the atmosphere from the inner vacuum of Orbitsville. The vessel's ion tubes and short-term reaction motors were effective against the weak pull of the shell, and it was possible for the *Bissendorf* to skip along the upper fringes of the air shield, gradually shedding velocity. It was even possible, using the fading reserves of reaction mass, to bring the ship down in one piece, with no further loss of life.

What was manifestly impossible, however, was to make the ship fly again.

All its external sensors had been seared cleanly from the hull, and many of the internal position-fixing devices had been destroyed or confused by the unnatural physics of Orbitsville. But the clocks were still in operation – and they had recorded a time lapse of five days. Five days from the passage through the Beachhead City aperture to the final touchdown on a hillside far into the interior. Starting from that basic fact, and using only a pocket calculator, it took just a few seconds for those on board to realize that they had travelled a distance of more than fifteen million kilometres.

In terms of the overall size of Orbitsville the journey was infinitesimal. A short hop, a stone's throw, a stroll across sunlit grass and woodlands – but in human terms the distance itself was more of a barrier than mountains or torrents. It was known, for instance, that back on Earth many a country postman had in his lifetime walked a total distance equal to a trip to the Moon, but that was only 385,000 kilometres. Walking back to Beachhead City would have been a task to be carried out by successive generations over a period of a thousand years.

Using the vast resources of the *Bissendorf*'s workshops it would have been possible to build a fleet of vehicles which might have cut the journey time down to a mere century –

except that wheels and other automobile components wear out in a matter of months. It would not be possible to transport the maintenance and manufacturing facilities which might have enabled the caravan to complete its golden journey.

There was also the difficulty that no man or machine knew the exact direction in which to travel. It would have been possible to get a rough bearing from the angle of the day and night ribs across the sky, but a rough bearing would be of no value. At the distances involved, a deviation of only one degree would have caused the train to miss Beachhead City by hundreds of thousands of sun-gleaming kilometres.

By the time the dead had been buried, the day was well advanced, and the remaining men and women of the *Bissendorf*'s crew were ceasing to be citizens of Earth. They were experiencing the infinity-change, the wistful, still contentment which poured down from the motionless sun of Orbitsville.

> *... that calm Sunday that goes on and on;*
> *When even lovers find their peace at last,*
> *And Earth is but a star, that once had shone.*

fourteen

'We're going back,' Garamond announced flatly.

He studied the faces of his executive staff, noting how they were reacting. Some looked at him with open amusement, others stared downwards into the grass, seemingly embarrassed. Behind them, further along the hillside, the great scarred hulk of the *Bissendorf* shocked the eye with its incongruity, and beyond it microscopic figures moved on the plain in the rituals of a ball game. The sun was directly overhead, as always, creating only an occasional flicker of diamond-fire on the dark blue waters of the lakes which banded the middle distance. Garamond began to feel that his words had been absorbed by Orbitsville's green infinities, sucked up cleanly before they reached the edge of the irregular ring in which the group was sitting, but he resisted the urge to repeat himself.

'It's a hell of a long way,' Napier said, finally breaking the heavy silence. His statement of the obvious, Garamond knew, constituted a question.

'We'll build aircraft.'

O'Hagan cleared his throat. 'I've already thought of that, Vance. We have enough workshop facilities still intact to manufacture a reasonable subsonic aircraft, and the micropedia can give us all the design data, but the distance is just too great. You run into exactly the same problem as with wheeled vehicles. Your aircraft might do the trip in three or four years – except that we haven't the resources to build a plane which can fly continuously for that length of time. And we couldn't transport major repair facilities.' O'Hagan glanced solemnly around the rest of the group, reproving them for having left it to him to deal with a wayward non-scientist.

Garamond shook his head. 'When I said we are going back, I didn't mean all of us, in a body. I meant that *I* am going back, together with any of the crew who are sufficiently determined to make it – even if that means only half-a-dozen of us.'

'But . . .'

'We're going to build a fleet of perhaps ten aircraft. We're going to incorporate as much redundancy as is compatible with good aerodynamics. We're going to fly our ten machines towards Beachhead City, and each time one of them breaks down we're going to take the best components out of it and put them in the other machines, and we're going to fly on.'

'There's no guarantee you'll get there, even with the last aircraft.'

'There's no guarantee I won't.'

'I'm afraid there is.' O'Hagan's pained expression had become even more pronounced. 'There's this problem of direction which we have already discussed. Unless you've got a really accurate bearing on Beachhead City there's no point in setting out.'

'I'm not worried about getting a precise bearing,' Garamond said, making a conscious decision to be enigmatic. He was aware that in the very special circumstances of the *Bissendorf*'s final flight the whole concept of command structure, of the captain-and-crew relationship, could easily lose its validity. It was necessary at this stage to re-establish himself in office without the aid of insignia or outside authority.

'How do you propose to get one ?'

'I propose instructing my science staff to attend to that chore for me. There's an old saying about the pointlessness of owning a dog and doing your own barking.' Garamond fixed a steady challenging gaze on O'Hagan, Sammy Yamoto, Morrison, Schneider and Denise Serra. He noted with satisfaction that they were responding as he had hoped – already there were signs of abstraction, of withdrawal to a plateau of thought upon which they became hunters casting nets for a quarry they had never seen but would recognize at first sight.

'While they're sorting that one out,' Garamond continued, speaking to Napier before any of the science staff could voice objections, 'we'll convene a separate meeting of the engineering committee. The ship has to be cut up to get the workshop floors level, but in the meantime I want the design definition drawn up for the aircraft and the first production tapes prepared.' He got to his feet and walked towards the improvised plastic hut he was using as an office. Napier, walking beside him, gave a dry cough which was out of place issuing from the barrel of his chest.

'TB again ?' Garamond said with mock sympathy.

'I think you're going too fast, Vance. Concentrating too much on the nuts and bolts, and not thinking enough about the human element.'

'Be more specific, Cliff.'

'A lot of the crew have got the Orbitsville syndrome already. They don't see any prospect of getting back to Beachhead City, and many of them don't even want to get back. They see no reason why they shouldn't set up a community right here, using the *Bissendorf* as a mine for essential materials.'

Garamond stopped, shielded his eyes and looked beyond the ship towards the plot of land, marked with a silver cross, where forty men and women had been buried. 'I can understand their feelings, and I'm not proposing to ride herd on those who want to stay. We'll use volunteers only.'

'There could be less than you expect.'

'Surely some of them, a lot of them, have reasons for getting back.'

'The point is that you aren't proposing to take them back, Vance. The planes won't make it all the way, so you're asking them to choose between staying here in a strong sizeable community with resources of power, materials and food – or being dropped somewhere between here and Beachhead City in groups of ten or less with very little to get them started as independent communities.'

'Each plane will have to carry an iron cow and a small plastics plant.'

'It's still a hell of a lot to ask.'

'I'll also guarantee that a rescue mission will set out as soon as I get back.'

'If you get back.'

A dark thought crossed Garamond's mind. 'How about you, Cliff? Are you coming with me?'

'I'm coming with you. All I'm trying to do is make you realize there's more to this than finding the right engineering approach.'

'I realize that already, but right now I've got all the human problems I can handle.'

'Others have wives and families they want to get back to.'

'That's the point – I haven't.'

'But . . .'

'How long do you think Aileen and Chris will survive after I'm presumed dead? A week? A day?' Garamond forced himself to speak steadily, despite the grief which kept up a steady thundering inside his head. 'The only reason I'm going back is that I have to kill Liz Lindstrom.'

*

Although it had been equipped and powered to carry out one emergency landing on the surface of a planet, the *Bissendorf* was in a supremely unnatural condition when beached with its longitudinal axis at right angles to the pull of gravity. The interior layout was based on the assumption that, except during short spells of weightlessness, there would be acceleration or retardation which would enable the crew to regard the prow as pointing 'upwards' and to walk normally on all its levels. Now the multitudinous floors of the vessel had become vertical walls to which were attached, in surrealistic attitudes, clusters of consoles, pedestals, desks, chairs, lockers, beds, tables and several hundred machines of varying types and capabilities. Because design allowance had been made for periods of free-fall – most small items, including paperwork, were magnetically or physically clamped in position – very little material had fallen to the lowermost side of the hull, but many of the ship's resources could not be tapped until key areas were properly orientated to the ground.

Teams of forcemasters using valency cutters and custom-built derricks began slicing the *Bissendorf*'s structure into manageable sections and rotating them to horizontal positions. The work was slowed down by the need to sever and reconnect power channels, but within a week the cylinder of the central hull had been largely converted into a cluster of low circular or wedge-shaped buildings. Each was roofed with a plastic diaphragm and linked by cable to power sources on the ground or within the butchered ship. The entire complex was surrounded by an umbra of tents and extemporized plastic sheds which gave it the appearance of an army encampment.

Garamond had placed maximum priority on the design and workshop facilities which were to create his aircraft, and the work was advancing with a speed which would have been impossible even a century earlier. The assembly line was already visible as nine sets of landing skids surmounted by the sketchy cruciforms of the basic airframes.

After weighing all considerations, the computers from the spaceship had decreed that the stressed-skin principle of aircraft construction, universal to aviation, should be abandoned in favour of the frame-and-fabric techniques employed in the Wright Brothers era. This permitted most of the high technology and engineering subtlety to be concentrated in a dozen pieces of alloy per ship, and the tape-controlled radiation millers hewed these from fresh billets in less than a day. The plastic skinning could then be carried out to the standards of a good quality furniture shop, and the engines – standard magnetic pulse prime movers – fitted straight from the shelf. It was the availability of engines, of which there were twenty-one in the *Bissendorf*'s inventory, which had been the main parameter in deciding upon a fleet of nine twin-engined ships which would set out upon the journey with three powerplants in reserve.

*

Garamond, sitting alone in the prismatic twilight at the entrance to his tent, was halfway through a bottle of whisky when he heard someone approaching. The nights never became truly dark under the striped canopy of Orbitsville's sky, and he was able to recognize the compact figure of Denise Serra while she was still some distance away. His annoyance at being disturbed faded somewhat but he sat perfectly still, making no sign of welcome. The whisky was his guarantee of sleep and to bring about the desired effect it had to be taken in precise rhythmic doses, with no interruptions to the ritual. Denise reached the tent, stood without speaking for a moment while she assessed his mood, then sat in the grass at the opposite side of the entrance. Appreciating her silence, Garamond waited till his instincts prompted him to take another measure of the spirit's cool fire. He raised the bottle to his lips.

'Drinking that can't be good for you,' Denise said.

'On the contrary – it's very good for me.'

'I never got to like whisky. Especially the stuff Burton makes.'

Garamond took his slightly delayed drink. 'It's all right if you know how to use it.'

'Use it ? Aren't you supposed to enjoy it ?'

'It's more important to me to know how to use it.'

She sighed. 'I'm sorry. I've heard about your wife being . . .'

'What did you want, Denise?'

'A child, I think.'

Garamond knew himself to have been rendered emotionally sterile by despair for his family, but he still retained enough contact with the mainstream of humanity to feel obliged to cap his bottle and set it aside.

'It's a bad time,' he said.

'I know, but that's the way I feel. It must be this place. It must be the Orbitsville syndrome that Cliff keeps talking about. We're here, and it's all around us, for ever, and things I used to think important now seem trivial. And, for the first time in my life, I want a child.'

Garamond stared at the girl through the veils of soft blue air, and a part of his mind – despite the pounding chaos of the rest – was intensely aware of her. It was difficult to pick out a single special attribute of Denise Serra, but the overall effect was right. She was a neat, complete package of femininity, intelligence and warmth, and he felt ashamed of having nothing to offer her.

'It's still a bad time,' he repeated.

'I know. We all know that, but some of the other women are drinking untreated water. It's only a matter of time till they become pregnant.' Her eyes watched him steadily and he remembered how, in that previous existence, it had given him pleasure to look at her.

'Haven't you already got a partner, Denise?'

'You know I haven't.'

That's it into the open, he thought. *For me to know that Denise Serra, among all the other female crew members, had no liaisons I would have to have been taking a special interest in her.*

'I guess I did know.' Garamond hesitated. 'Denise, I feel . . .'

'Honoured?'

'I think that's the word I would have used.'

'Say no more, Vance. I know what it means when somebody starts off by feeling honoured. I've done it myself.' She stood up in one easy movement.

Garamond tried for something less abrupt, and knew he was being clumsy. 'Perhaps in a year, a few months . . .'

'The special unrepeatable offer will be closed before then,' Denise said with an uncharacteristic harshness in her voice. 'Have you thought about what you're going to do if we can't get a bearing on Beachhead City, if your flight never gets off the ground?'

'I'm counting on your getting that bearing.'

'Don't!' She turned quickly, walked away for a few paces, then came back and knelt close to him. 'I'm sorry, Vance.'

'You haven't done anything to apologize for.'

'I think I have. You see, we've pretty well solved the problem. Dennis O'Hagan didn't want to say anything to you till he'd made a check on the math.'

'But . . .' Garamond's attention was fully captured. 'How is it going to be done?'

'Mike Moncaster, our particles man, came up with the idea. You know about delta particles?'

'I've heard of delta rays.'

'No, that's historic stuff. Delta particles – deltons – are a component of cosmic rays discovered only a few years ago. During his last leave Mike got himself seconded on to the team investigating cosmic ray refraction by the force field which seals Beachhead City aperture. They were glad to have him because he's pretty good on the Conservation of Strangeness and . . .'

'Denise! You started to tell me how you were going to get a bearing.'

'That's what I'm doing. Deltons don't interact much. That's why it took so long to find them, but it also means they could travel ten or fifteen million kilometres through the air. Mike is fairly certain they get refracted by the force lens, just like other components of cosmic rays, so we're going to build a big delton detector. Two of them, in fact. One behind the other to give us co-ordinates. All we need then is to pick up a delton, just one, and going back the way it came will give us a straight line home.'

'Do you think it'll work?'

'I think so.' Denise's voice was kind. 'What we still have to determine is how long we're likely to wait before a particle comes this way. It could be quite a while if things aren't in our favour, but we can swing the odds by making the detectors as big as possible, or by erecting a whole bank of them.'

Garamond felt the distance between himself and Elizabeth Lindstrom shrink a little and the joyful sickness spurted within him. 'This . . . is good news.'

'I know,' Denise said. 'My dowry.'

'You'll have to explain that one.'

'The first time you ever noticed me was on board ship, when I gave the news you wanted to hear about going through the aperture.' She laughed ruefully. 'Being a pragmatist, I must have decided that if it worked once it would work again.'

Garamond moved his hand uncertainly in the dimness and touched her cheek. 'Denise, I . . .'

'Let's not play games, Vance.' She pushed his hand away and stood up. 'I was childish, that's all.'

Later, while waiting for sleep to relieve him of the burden of identity, Garamond was acutely aware – for the first time in months – that the hard, angry vacuum of space began only a short distance beneath his cot. The feeling persisted into surrealistic dreams in which he had a sense of being poised, dangerously, on the rim of a precipice, with a kind of moral vertigo drawing him over the edge.

fifteen

On his way to the airstrip Garamond was surprised to notice one of his crewmen wearing what could only be described as a coolie hat. He eyed the young man curiously, received a half-hearted salute, and decided the unusual headgear must be a personal souvenir of a tourist trip to the Orient. A minute later, while passing the workshop area, he saw two more men wearing similar hats, which he now realized were woven from fresh silver-green straw. The ancient peasant-styling, with all that it symbolized in Earth's history, was repugnant to Garamond and he hoped it would not become a full-blown fad such as occasionally swept through the crew levels. When he reached the test site, the glinting of flat green triangles in the distance told him that coolie hats were being worn by at least half the men who were clearing grass at the far end of the airstrip.

Cliff Napier was waiting for him at the door to the operations shed, his shoulder-heavy bulk filling the entrance. 'Morning, Vance. We're nearly ready to fly.'

'Good.' Garamond eyed the first aircraft appraisingly then turned his gaze back along the strip. 'It looks like a paddy field down there – why are the men wearing those sunhats?'

'Would you believe,' Napier said impassively, 'to protect them from the sun?'

'But why that sort of hat?' Garamond ignored the sarcasm.

'I guess it's because they're light and easy to make. And it's a good shape if the sun's directly above you and you're working in the dirt all day.'

'I still don't like them.'

'You're not working in the dirt all day.' This time there was no mistaking the coldness in the big man's manner.

Garamond locked eyes with Napier and was shaken to feel a momentary surge of anger and dislike. *This can't be*, he thought. Aloud he said, 'Do you expect me to? Do you think I'm not making the most efficient use of human resources?'

'From your point of view, you are.'

'And from their point of view?'

'The cold season's coming down soon. Most of the crew are staying here, remember. They'd rather be building houses and processing grass into protein cakes.'

Garamond decided against answering immediately in case he damaged a working relationship. He glanced up at the sky and saw that, behind the shield of brilliance, the broadest ribs of light blue were well in the ascendant in the west. They signified that summer was approaching the diametrically opposite point on Orbitsville's shell, that Autumn was ending on the near side.

'This Orbitsville syndrome of yours,' he said after a pause. 'An early symptom is that a man develops an aversion to taking orders, right?'

'That seems to come into it.'

'Then let's sit down together and agree a common set of goals. That way . . .'

'That way we'd do everything you want and you wouldn't even have to give the orders,' Napier said sharply, but this time he was smiling.

Garamond smiled in return. 'Why do you think I suggested it?' Although the little crisis had passed, he had a feeling it carried significance for the future and he was determined to take appropriate action. 'We'll open a bottle tonight and get our ideas straightened out.'

'I thought we were out of whisky.'

'No. There's plenty.'

'You're on the stuff that Burton makes?'

'Why not?'

An incongruous primness appeared briefly on Napier's dark features. 'Maybe we can fix something up later. How about looking at this airplane?'

'Certainly.' They walked out towards the waiting machine which was the biscuit colour of unpainted plastic. It was a high-wing monoplane, sitting nose-high on its skids and looking like something from a museum of aeronautics, but Garamond had no doubts about its capabilities. The ungainly ship would carry a crew of five at a maximum cruise of five hundred kilometres an hour for fifty days at a stretch, landing after that time to replenish food and water. Even this limitation was forced on it by the fact that more than two-thirds of the payload would be taken up by spares, an iron cow and other supplies.

Garamond glanced from the newly completed machine to the others of its kind further back on the open-air production line, and from them up to the black rectangular screen of the delton detector on the hillside. He felt a vague spasm of alarm over the extent to which his future was dependent on complex artifacts, but this was obliterated by the yearning hunger which kept him alive and was the motive force behind all his actions. It was ironic, he had often thought in the hours before sleep, how – in depriving him of all that was worth living for in his previous life – Elizabeth Lindstrom had provided, in herself, the single goal of his new existence. She had also given him the means of escaping from it, for he could foresee no way of long surviving the act of pulling the President's ribcage apart with his bare hands and gripping the heaving redness within and . . .

'I know what you're thinking, Vance.'

'Do you ?' Garamond stared into the face of the stranger who had spoken to him, and he made the effort which allowed him to associate it with Cliff Napier. There was a psychic wrench and once again he was back into the sane world, walking towards the aircraft with his senior officer.

'Well, don't keep me in suspense,' he heard himself saying.

'I think you're secretly pleased the electronics lab isn't able to build autopilots. If we're going to fly that distance we want to *fly* it. We want to be able to tell people we did it with our hands.'

Garamond nodded. *With our hands,* he thought. One of the group standing at the plane was wearing a coolie hat and when its owner turned to greet him Garamond was startled to see the sweat-beaded features of Troy Litman, the senior production executive. Litman was a short pudgy man who had always compensated for the natural untidiness of his physique by paying strict attention to his uniform and off-duty dress, and he was one of the last Garamond would have expected to favour a badly-woven grass hat. Garamond began to doubt his earlier conviction that the design of the grass headgear was symbolic rather than utilitarian.

'The ship looks good,' Garamond said. 'Is she ready to fly ?'

'As near as she'll ever be.'

Like the hat, the answer was not what Garamond would have expected of Litman. 'How near is that ?'

'Relax, Vance.' Litman grinned within the column of shadow projected by the brim of his hat. 'That ship will take you as far as you want to go.'

'I'm ready to take her up now, sir,' Braunek said opportunely, from the opposite side of the group.

'You're happy enough about it ?'

'If the computer's happy I'm happy, sir. Anyway I did a few fast taxis yesterday and she felt fine.'

'Go ahead, then.' Garamond watched the young man climb into the plane's glasshouse and strap himself into his seat. A few seconds later the propellers started to turn, silently driven by the magnetic resonance engines, and the control surfaces flicked in anticipation. As the propeller revolutions built up the group moved out of the backwash and a similar scattering took place among the work gangs at the far end of the runway. The plane began to move and several excited shouts went up, signifying that, despite the computer predictions and tape-controlled machines, there had remained some areas of human participation.

In its unloaded condition the aircraft used very little of the runway before lifting cleanly into the air. It continued in a straight line for about a kilometre, rising steadily, shadow flitting over the grass directly below, then banked into a lazy turn and circled the encampment. The soundless flight seemed effortless, like that of a gull riding on a fresh breeze, but on the third pass Garamond thought he saw a small object detach itself from the aircraft and go fluttering to the ground.

'What was that ?' Napier said, screening his eyes. 'I saw something fall '

'Nothing fell,' Litman asserted very quickly.

'I saw something too,' Garamond put in. 'You'd better get a medic on to the truck, just in case.'

'It wouldn't do any good – we had to pull the transmission out.'

'What ?' Garamond stared in disbelief at Litman's uneasy but defiant face. 'One of the first basic procedures we agreed was that the truck would be kept at readiness during flight testing.'

'I guess I forgot.'

Garamond flicked a hand upwards, sending Litman's hat tumbling behind him. 'You are not a peasant,' he said harshly.

'You are not a coolie. You are a Starflight executive officer and I'm going to see that you . . .'

'Braunek's coming back,' someone said and Garamond returned his attention to the aircraft. The pilot had not tried, or had been unable, to line up on the runway but was coming in parallel to it, his ship rising and sinking noticeably as it breasted the wind. Garamond estimated the touchdown point and relaxed slightly as he saw it would be well to the north of the buildings and tents which were clustered around the hulk of the *Bissendorf*. The plane continued its descent, side-slipping a little but holding fairly well to its course.

'I told you there was nothing to worry about,' Litman said in a reproachful voice.

'You'd better be right.' Garamond kept his eyes on Braunek's ship. The side-slipping was more noticeable now, but each skid brought the plane a little closer to the centreline of the cleared strip and Garamond hoped that Braunek was good enough at his trade to be doing it on purpose. He knew, however, that there had to come a moment, a precise moment, in every air crash when the spectator on the ground was forced to accept that the pilot had lost his struggle against the law of aerial physics, that a disaster had to occur. For Garamond, the moment came when he saw that the starboard propeller was ceasing to spin. The plane pulled to the right, as though the wing on that side had hit an invisible pylon, and it staggered down the perilous sky towards the hillside. Towards, Garamond suddenly realized, the black rectangle of the delton detector. He was unable to breathe during the final few seconds of flight as the doomed ship, see-sawing its wings, became silhouetted against land instead of sky and then flailed its way through the delton screen. And it was not until the sound of the crash reached him that he was freed from his stasis and began to run.

*

Braunek's life was saved by the fact that the lightweight frames of the detector screens served as efficient absorbers of kinetic energy. They had accepted the impact, folding almost gently around the ship, stretching and twisting, and then trailing out behind it like vines. By the time Garamond reached the location of the crash Braunek had been helped out of the wreckage and was sitting on the grass. He was surrounded by technicians who had been working in and had run out of the small hut linked to the screens, and one of them was spraying tissue sealant over a gash on his leg.

'I'm glad you made it,' Garamond said, feeling inadequate. 'How do you feel?'

Braunek shook his head. '*I'm* all right, but everything else is screwed up.' He tried to raise himself from the ground.

Garamond pushed him back. 'Don't move. I want the medics to have a proper look at you. What happened anyway?'

'Starboard wing centre panel dropped off.'

'It just *dropped* off?'

Braunek nodded. 'It took the engine control runs with it, otherwise I could have brought the ship in okay.'

Garamond jumped to his feet. 'Litman! Find that panel and bring it here. *Fast!*'

Litman, who was just arriving on the scene, looked exasperated but he turned without a word and ran back down the hillside. Garamond stayed talking with Braunek until a medic arrived to check him over, then he surveyed the ruins of the delton screen. Somewhere in the middle of the wreckage a damaged aircraft engine was still releasing gyromagnetic impulses which sent harmless flickers of detuned energy racing over the metalwork like St Elmo's fire. Where accidental resonances occurred a feeble motive force was conjured up and the broken struts of the framework twitched like the legs of a dying insect. The destruction looked final to Garamond but he checked with O'Hagan and confirmed that the screen had been rendered useless except as a source of raw materials.

'How long till you have another one operational?'

'A week perhaps,' O'Hagan said. 'We'll go for modular construction this time. That means we could have small areas operational in a couple of days, and we could build up to a useful size before your airplanes are ready to take off.'

'Do that.' Garamond left his Chief Science Officer staring

gloomily into the wreckage and went down the hillside to meet the group which had retrieved the lost wing section. The men set the plastic panel down in front of him and stood back without speaking. Garamond ran his gaze over it and saw at once that the two longitudinal edges which should have been ridged with welding overlays were square and clean except for small positioning welds which had broken.

Garamond turned to face Litman. 'All right – who was responsible for the welding of this panel, and who was supposed to inspect?'

'It's hard to say,' Litman replied.

'Hard to say?'

'That's what I said.'

'Then check it out on the work cards.' Garamond spoke with insulting gentleness.

'What work cards?' Litman, suddenly tired of being pushed, turned a red, resentful face up to Garamond's. 'Where have you been, Mister Garamond? Did nobody tell you we've only got bits of a workshop left? Did nobody tell you that winter's coming and we just can't *afford* all the time and material that's going into these flying toys of yours?'

'That isn't in your area of competence.'

'Of course not!' The redness had spread into Litman's eyes as he glanced around the gathering crowd. 'I'm only a production man. I'm just one of the slobs who has to meet your airy-fairy target dates with no bloody equipment. But there's something you seem to forget, Mister Garamond. Out here a man who knows how to use his hands is worth twenty Starflight commanders who have nothing left to command.'

'What'll you do if we decide not to finish your planes?' A low, interested murmur arose from the men behind Litman.

Cliff Napier stepped into the arena. 'For a so-called production man,' he said, 'you seem to do a lot of work with your mouth, Litman. I suggest that you . . .'

'It's all right,' Garamond cut in, placing a restraining hand on Napier's arm. He raised his voice so that he could be heard by everybody in the vicinity. 'I know how most of you feel about settling down here and making the best of things. And I know you want to get on with survival work before the weather turns. Furthermore, I can sympathize with your point of view about obsolescent Starflight commanders – but let me assure you of one thing. I'm leaving here with a fleet of airplanes, and the airplanes are going to be built properly, to the very highest standards of which we are capable. If I find they don't work as well as they ought to I'll simply turn them around and fly them right back to you.

'So the only way – the *only* way – you'll get me out of your hair permanently is by building good airplanes. And don't come sniffling to me about target dates or shortage of equipment. Don't forget – I've seen how you can work when you feel like it. What sort of a target date did we have when we were getting ready to punch a hole right through the middle of Beachhead City?' Garamond paused and out-stared the man nearest to him.

'A nice finishing touch,' Napier whispered. 'If they still have pride.'

'Ah, hell,' somebody growled from several rows back. 'We might as well finish the job now we've done most of the work.' There was a general rumble of assent and the crowd, after a moment's hesitation, began to disperse. The response was not as wholehearted as Garamond could have wished for, but he felt a sense of relief at having secured any kind of decision over Litman. The production executive, his face expressionless, was turning away with the others.

'Troy,' Garamond said to him, 'we could have talked that one out in private.'

Litman shrugged. 'I'm satisfied with the way things went.'

'Are you? You used to be known as the best production controller in the S.E.A. fleet.'

'That's all in the past, Vance. I've got bigger things on my mind now.'

'Bigger than a man's life? Braunek could have been killed over that sloppy workmanship.'

'I'm sorry about young Braunek getting hurt, and I'm glad he's all right.' Litman paused and retraced his steps towards

Garamond. 'The reason the men went along with you a moment ago is that you gave them Orbitsville – and that's important to them. They're going to spread out through Orbitsville, Vance. This camp won't hold together more than a year or two, and then most likely it will be left empty.'

'We were talking about the plane crash.'

'We don't stand united any more. Any man who trusts his life to a machine he hasn't made by himself and personally checked out by himself is a fool. You should remember that.' Litman turned and plodded away down the hillside, probably intent on retrieving his coolie hat. Garamond stared after the compact figure, filled with the uneasy dislike that a man always feels for another who seems in closer touch with the realities of a situation. He thought hard about Litman's words during the midday meal and as a result decided to turn himself into a one-man inspection and quality assurance team, with entire responsibility for the airworthiness of his aircraft.

The self-imposed task – with its round of visual and physical checking of every aspect of the fleet production – occupied nine-tenths of Garamond's working hours, and brought the discovery that he still retained the ability to sleep without stunning his system with alcohol.

*

Garamond was spreadeagled across the tailplane of the seventh aircraft, examining the elevator hinges, when he felt a tap on his shoulder. It was late in the day and therefore hot – temperatures on Orbitsville built up steadily throughout each daylight period, before dropping abruptly at nightfall – and he had been hoping to finish the particular job without interruption. He kept his head inside the resinous darkness of the inspection hatch, hoping the interloper would take the hint and go away, but there came another and more insistent tap. Garamond twisted into a sitting position and found himself looking into the creased dry face of O'Hagan. The scientist had never been a happy-looking man but on this occasion his expression was more bleak than usual, and Garamond felt a stab of concern.

He switched off his inspection light and slid to the ground. 'Has anything happened, Dennis?'

O'Hagan gave a reluctant nod. 'We've recorded a delta particle.'

'You've recorded a . . .' Garamond pressed the back of his hand to his forehead and fought to control his elation. 'Isn't that what we've been trying to do ? What's your worry ?'

'We've only got about eighty per cent of the original screen rebuilt.'

'So ?'

'It's too soon, Vance. I've been through Mike Moncaster's math a couple of times and I can't fault him. With two complete screens – which is what we planned for – giving a receiving area of five hundred square metres, we should have had to wait eighty or ninety days even to . . .'

'We were lucky,' Garamond interrupted, laughing and astonished to realize he still remembered how. 'It just shows that the laws of probability are bound to give you a break eventually. Come on, Dennis, admit it.'

O'Hagan shook his head with sombre conviction. 'The laws of probability are not bound to give you anything, my friend.'

*

The eight aircraft took off at first light, while the air was cool and thick, and climbed steadily against the seriate blue archways of the Orbitsville sky. At the agreed cruising height of five hundred metres the ungainly, stiff-winged birds levelled off, exchanging brief communications through pulses of modulated light. They assumed a V-formation, and circled once around the base camp, their shadows falling vertically on to the remains of the *Bissendorf*, the metallic egg which had brought about their slow and painful birth. And then, without lingering further, they set course towards the prismatic mists which lay to the east.

sixteen

Day 8. Estimated range: 94,350 kilometres

For a start, I am determined to avoid the abbreviations traditionally used by diarists – their function is that of shortening a necessary task, whereas my aim is to prolong a superfluous one. (The term 'ship's log' might be more appropriate than 'diary'; but, again, the log is a record of the events of a voyage, whereas the daily entries in my book are likely to be the only pseudo-events in a continuum of pure monotony.) (If I go on splitting hairs like this about the precise meanings of words in the opening sentence, I'll never get beyond it; but the reference to abbreviations isn't quite right, either. I intend to use the symbol 'O' instead of writing out 'Orbitsville' in full each time. O is much shorter than Orbitsville, but that is coincidental – it is also more expressive of the reality.)

Cliff Napier was right when he guessed I was glad the job of manufacturing autopilots was beyond our resources. My reasoning was that flying the ship by hand would keep us occupied and help to reduce the boredom. It isn't working out that way, though. There are five of us on board and we spell each other at the controls on a rota which is arranged so that the two most experienced pilots – Braunek and myself – are in the cockpit at daybreak and nightfall. These are the only times when flying the ship becomes more difficult than driving an automobile. Because day and night are caused by bands of light and darkness sweeping over the land at orbital speed, there is no proper dawn and no proper dusk, and some fairly violent meteorological processes take place.

In the 'morning' a sector of cold air which has been sinking steadily for hours suddenly finds itself warming up again and rising, causing anything from clear air turbulence to heavy rain. At nightfall the situation is reversed but can be even more tricky because the air which cools and begins to descend conflicts with currents rising from the still-warm ground.

143

All it amounts to, however, is that there are two half-hour periods when the control column comes to life. Not enough to occupy us for the next three to four years, I'm afraid, although we in the lead ship are a little luckier than the others in having a little extra work to do. There is the inertial course reference to be monitored, for instance. It is a simple-looking black box, created by O'Hagan and his team, and inside it is a monomaniac electronic brain which thinks of nothing but the bearing they fed into it. Any time we begin to wander off course a digital counter instructs us to go left or right till we're back on line again, and the rest of the squadron follows suit.

Linked to the black box there is a one-metre-square delton detector which in a year or two, as we get considerably closer to Beachhead City, should begin to pick up other delta particles and provide course confirmation. Sometimes I watch it, just in case, or just to pass the time, but there isn't really any need. It would feed a fresh bearing into the course reference automatically, and is also fitted with an audio attention-getter. I still watch it, though . . . and dream about EL. No abbreviations – Elizabeth Lindstrom.

Day 23. Estimated range: 278,050 kilometres

We've completed perhaps a fortieth of the journey, having flown a distance roughly equivalent to going round the Earth seven times. Without stopping. Another way to reckon it is that, after 23 days, we've gone nearly as far as a ray of light would have travelled in one second, but that's a depressing thought to anyone who has been accustomed to Arthurian flight at multiples of light-speed. A more positive thought is that we've learned quite a lot about O.

Somehow, I'd always thought of it as being composed entirely of featureless prairie, but I was wrong. Perhaps it started off that way, eons ago, and the subsequent action of wind led to the formation of the mountains we've seen. None of them was very high, not more than a couple of thousand metres, but with the land area of five billion Earths not yet explored who's to say what will be found? The mountains are there, anyway, and some of them are capped with snow because our flight is taking us into the winter sector, and there are rivers and small seas. Our formation passes over them in a dead straight line, quietly and steadily, and sometimes the telescopes pick up herds of grazing animals. Perhaps settlers will not have to rely exclusively on vegetable protein, after all.

The unexpected variegation of the terrain is making the journey a little easier to endure, but after a time all seas are the same, all hills look alike . . .

When I wrote in an earlier entry that the five of us in the lead ship were luckier than the others in having more to do, I was not thinking about the members of the science staff. Sammy Yamoto in No 4 seems to be fully occupied with astronomical readings, including precise measurements of the width of the day and night bands as we cross them, or as they cross us. He now says that, even with improvised equipment, he could probably take a bearing on Beachhead City which would be accurate to within a degree or so. I suspect he is passing up his turn at the flying controls so that he can carry on with his work. I hope this is not the case, because he is one of the least expert pilots and needs the practice. Although five per ship is ample crew strength, this could be cut down, by illness, for example, and I'm making no provision for unscheduled stops. Any ships which have to go down for long periods will be stripped and left behind. With their crews.

Cliff Napier in No 2 is filling in free time by helping Denise Serra in a series of experiments connected with recording radiation and gravity fluctuations.

Sometimes – in fact, quite often – I find myself wishing Denise was on my ship. I could have arranged it at the start, of course, but I wanted to play fair with her. Having turned her down that night, I felt the least I could do was avoid obstructing the field. But now . . . Now when I dream about Aileen and Chris I dream they are dead, which means I'm beginning to accept it, and with the acceptance my pragmatic, faithless body seems to be nominating Aileen's successor. I feel ashamed about this, but perhaps it is not as purely physical as I was supposing.

Delia Liggett, who was a catering supervisor on the *Bissendorf*, is on my ship and two of the other men have a good practical relationship with her – but I can't work up much interest in a hot bunking system. I'm positive this isn't a ridiculous remnant of a captain-to-crew attitude, a notion that I ought to have her exclusively because I had the most silver braid on my uniform.

Outside the agreed goals of this mission I have, probably with some assistance from the pervading influence of the Big O, completely discarded the old command structure. I do remember, though, feeling some surprise at the make-up of the thirty-nine volunteers who came with me. My first supposition was that they would all be of executive rank and above, career-oriented men and women who were determined to take the *Bissendorf* incident in their stride. Instead, I found that over half of the seventy original volunteers were ordinary crewmen. Those who remained, after the selection procedure which cut the number down to the precise requirement, I regard and treat as exact equals.

O makes us equal.

In comparison to it we are reduced to the ultimate, human electrons, too small to admit of any disparity in size.

Day 54. Estimated range: 620,000 kilometres

We have completed our first scheduled landing and are in flight again. After fifty days in the air, the prospect of three days on the ground was exhilarating. We landed in formation on a level plain, the eight fully qualified pilots at the controls, and spent practically all the down-time in gathering grass and loading it into the processing machines. This is what passes for winter on O. The sun is still directly overhead, naturally enough, but with the days being shorter the temperature does not build up as high and has a much longer time to bleed away at night. It results in nothing more than a certain briskness in the air during the day, although the nights are a lot colder. (It makes me wonder why the designers of O bothered to build in a mechanism to provide seasons. If the hostel-for-the-galaxy notion is correct, presumably the designers carried out a survey of intelligent life-forms in their region of space to see what the environmental requirements were. And if that is the case, the majority of life-bearing worlds must closely resemble Earth, even to the extent of having a moderately tilted axis and a procession of seasons. Could this, for some reason I don't fathom, be a universal pre-requisite for the evolution of intelligence?)

It seems that weather isn't going to be any problem during future stops, but our physical condition might. The simple task of cutting and gathering grass pretty well exhausted a lot of people, and now we are instituting programmes of exercises which can be performed on board ship.

Day 86. Estimated range: 1,038,000 kilometres

With more than a million kilometres behind us, it was beginning to look as though our journey time would be better than predicted, but the first hint of mechanical difficulties has shown up. The starboard propeller bearing on ship No 7 has started to show some wear. This is causing vibration at maximum cruise and we have had to reduce fleet speed by twelve kilometres per hour. The loss of speed is not very significant in itself, because it could be compensated for by extended engine life, but the alarming thing is that the propeller shaft bearings on all the ships are supposed to have been made in Magnelube Alloy Grade E. It is inconceivable that a bearing made to that specification could begin to show wear after only 83 days of continuous running – and the suspicion crosses my mind that Litman may have substituted Magnelube D, or even C. (I do not believe he would have done this out of pure malice, but if there was a shortage of blocks of the top grade metal and I had discovered it I would have ordered a redesign or would have stripped some of the *Bissendorf*'s main machinery to get the bearings. Either way, Litman would have had a lot of extra work on his hands, and the person he has become would not take kindly to that.) We must now keep a careful watch on all propeller shaft bearings because we carry no stocks of Magnelube Alloy and, in any case, barely retain the ability to machine it to the required tolerances. Like archaeologists burrowing deeper into the past, we are retrogressing through various levels of technical competence.

In the meantime, the flight continues uninterrupted. Over prairies, lakes, mountains, seas, forests – and then over more and more of the same. A million kilometres is an invisible fraction of O's circumference, and yet seeing it like this has stunned one part of my mind. I was taught at school that a man's brain is unable to comprehend what is meant by a light-year – now I know we cannot comprehend as much as a light-second. So far in this journey we have, in effect, encircled twenty-five Earths; but my heart and mind are suspended, like netted birds, somewhere above the third or fourth range of mountains. They have run into the comprehension barrier, while my body has travelled onwards, heedless of what penalties may fall due.

Day 93. Estimated range: 1,080,000 kilometres

Like Litman, like the others, I am becoming a different person.

I sometimes go for a whole day without thinking about Elizabeth Lindstrom. And now I can think about Aileen and Chris without experiencing much pain. It is as if they are in a mental jewel box. I can take them out of it, examine them, receive pleasure – then put them back into it and close the lid. The thought has occurred to me that the life of a loved one must be considered algebraically – setting the positive total of happiness and contentment against the negative quantity represented by pain and death. This process, even for a very short life, results in a positive expression. I wish I could discuss this idea with someone who might understand, but Denise is on another ship.

Day 109. Estimated range: 1,207,000 kilometres

We have lost Tayman's ship, No 6. It happened while we were landing for our second scheduled stop, putting down in formation on an ideal-looking plain. There was a hidden spar of rock which wrecked one of Tayman's skids, causing the plane to dip a wing. Nobody was hurt, but No 6 had to be written off.

(In future we will land in sequence on the lead aircraft's skid marks to reduce the risk of similar incidents.) Tayman and his crew – which includes two women – took the mishap philosophically and we spent an extra day on the ground getting them set up for a prolonged stay. Among the parts we took from No 6 were the propeller shaft bearings, one of which was immediately installed in No 7's starboard engine.

I suppose the latter has to be regarded as a kind of bonus – fleet speed is back to maximum cruise – but the loss of Jack Tayman's steady optimism is hard to accept. Strangely, I find myself missing his aircraft most at night. We have no radio altimeters or equivalents because the conditions on O will not permit electromagnetic transmission, and the environment also makes barometric pressure readings too unreliable, so we use the ancient device of two inclined spotlights on each aircraft, one at each end of the fuselage. The forward laser ray is coloured red, the aft one white, and they intersect at five hundred metres, which means that a machine flying at the chosen height projects a single pink spot. Looking downwards through the darkness we can see our V-formation slipping across the ground, hour after hour, a squadron of silent moons, and the disappearance of one of those luminous followers is all too apparent.

Day 140. Estimated range: 1,597,000 kilometres

Within the space of ten days propeller shaft bearing trouble has developed on five ships, and fleet speed has been reduced by fifty kilometres an hour. Prognosis is that there will be continued deterioration, with progressive cuts in flying speed. Everybody is properly dismayed, but I think I can detect an undercurrent of relief at the possibility of so many aircraft having to drop out at the same time, thus providing for the setting up of a larger and stronger community. I have discussed the situation with Cliff Napier over the lightphone and even he seems to be losing heart.

The only aspect of the matter which looks at all 'hopeful' is that the ships which have experienced the trouble are No 3 through to No 8, which reflects the order in which they came off the production line. The first and second ships – mine and Napier's – are all right, and it may be that Litman had enough Grade E metal available for our propeller bearings. I put the word hopeful in quotes in this context because, on reflection, it simply is not appropriate. Being reduced to two airplanes at this stage of the mission would be disastrous, and it would take fairly comprehensive technical resources to restore us to strength. Resources which are not available.

I am writing this at night, mainly because I can't sleep, and I find it difficult to fight off a sense of defeat. The Big O is too . . .

Garamond set his stylus aside as Joe Braunek, who had been in the cockpit serving as stand-by pilot, appeared in the gangway beside his bunk. The young man's face was deeply shadowed by the single overhead light tube but his eyes, within their panda-patches of darkness, were showing an abnormal amount of white.

'What is it, Joe ?' Garamond closed his diary.

'Well, sir . . .'

'Vance.'

'Sorry, I keep . . . Do you want to come up front a minute, Vance ?'

'This gets us back to square one – is there anything wrong ? I'm trying to rest and I don't want to get up without a good reason.'

'There are some lights we can't explain.'

'Which panel ?'

Braunek shook his head. 'Not that sort of light. Outside the ship – near the horizon. It looks like there's a city of some kind ahead of us.'

seventeen

At first sight, the lights were disappointing. Because the fleet was travelling roughly eastwards, the blue and darker blue bands which represented day and night on other parts of Orbitsville were arcing across the sky from side to side. The lower one looked in the eastern sky the narrower and closer together the bands appeared to grow, until they merged in the opalescent haze above the upcurving black horizon. Even when Braunek had shown him where to look Garamond had to scan the darkness for several seconds before he picked out a thin line of yellowish radiance, like a razor cut just below the edge of a cardboard silhouette.

Delia Liggett, who was at the controls, raised her face to him. 'Is there any chance that . . . ?'

'It isn't Beachhead City,' Garamond said. 'Let's get that clear.'

'I thought there might have been a mistake over distances.'

'Sorry, Delia. We're working on a very rough estimate of how far the *Bissendorf* travelled, but not that rough. You can start looking out for Beachhead City in earnest a couple of years from now.' There was silence in the cockpit except for the insistent rush of air against the sides of the ship.

'Then what is that ?'

Garamond perversely refused to admit excitement. 'It looks like sky reflections on a lake.'

'Wrong colour,' Braunek said, handing Garamond a pair of binoculars. 'Try these.'

'It has to be an alien settlement,' Garamond admitted as the glasses revealed the beaded brightness of a distant city. 'And it's so far from the entrance to the sphere.'

At that moment Cliff Napier's voice came through on the lightphone. 'Number Two speaking – is that Vance I can see in the cockpit ?'

'I hear you, Cliff.'

'Have you seen what we've seen?'

'Yeah – and are you wondering what I'm wondering?'

Napier hesitated. 'You mean, what's an alien city doing way out here? I guess they got to Orbitsville a very long time before we did. It might have taken them hundreds or thousands of years to drift out this far.'

'But why did they bother? You've seen what Orbitsville's like – one part is as good as another.'

'To us, Vance. Aliens could see things a different way.'

'I don't know,' Garamond said dubiously. 'You always say things like that.' He dropped into one of the supernumerary seats and fixed his eyes on the horizon, waiting for the wall of daylight to rush towards him from the east. When it came, about an hour later, sweeping over the ground with thought-paralysing speed, the alien settlement abruptly became an even less noticeable feature of the landscape. Although it was now within a hundred kilometres, the 'city' was reduced in the binoculars to a mere dusting of variegated dots almost lost in greenery. During the lightphone conversations between the air-craft there had been voiced the idea that it might be possible to obtain new propeller bearings or have the existing ones modi-fied. Garamond, without expressing any quick opinions on a subject so important to him, had been quietly hopeful about the aliens' level of technology – but his optimism began to fade. The community which hovered beyond the prow of his ship reminded him of a Nineteenth Century town in the American West.

'Looks pretty rustic to me.' Ralston, the telegeologist, had borrowed the glasses and was peering through them.

'Mark Twain land?'

'That's it.'

Garamond nodded. 'This is completely illogical, of course. We can't measure other cultures with our own yardstick, but I have a feeling that that's a low-technology agricultural com-munity up there. Maybe it's because I believe that any race which settles on Orbitsville will turn into farmers. There's no need for them to do anything else.'

'Hold on a minute, Vance.' Ralston's voice was taut. 'Maybe you're going to get those bearings, after all. I think I see an airplane.'

Numb with surprise, Garamond took the offered binoculars and aimed them where Ralston directed. After a moment's search he found a complicated white speck hanging purposefully in the lower levels of the air. The absence of any lateral movement suggested the other plane was flying directly away from or directly towards his own, and his intuition told him the latter was the case. He kept watching through the powerful, gyro-stabilized glasses and presently saw other motes of coloured brightness rising, swarming uncertainly, and then settling into the apparently motionless state which meant they were flying to meet him head-on. Ralston gave the alert to the six other ships of the fleet.

'It's a welcoming party, all right,' he said as the unknown planes became visible to the naked eye, 'and we've no weapons. What do we do if they attack us?'

'We have to assume they're friendly, or at least not hostile.' Garamond adjusted the fine focus on the binoculars. 'Besides – I know I'm judging them by our standards again – but that doesn't look like an air force to me. The planes are all different colours.'

'Like ancient knights going out to do battle.'

'Could be, but I don't think so. The planes seem to be pretty small, and all different types.' A stray thought crossed Garamond's mind. He turned his attention back to the city from which the planes had arisen, and was still scanning it with growing puzzlement when the two fleets of aircraft met and coalesced.

A green-and-yellow low-wing monoplane took up station beside Garamond's ship and wiggled its wings in what, thanks to the strictures of aerial dynamics, had to be the universal greeting of airmen. The alien craft had a small blister-type canopy through which could be seen a humanoid form. Braunek, now at the controls, laughed delightedly and repeated the signal. The tiny plane near their wingtip followed suit, as did a blue biplane beyond it.

'Communication!' Braunek shouted. 'They aren't like the Clowns, Vance – we'll be able to talk to these people.'

'Good. See if you can get their permission to land,' Garamond said drily.

'Right.' Braunek, unaware of the irony, became absorbed in making an elaborate series of gestures while Garamond twisted around in his seat to observe as many of the alien ships as he could. He had noted earlier that no two were painted alike; now he was able to confirm that they all differed radically in design. Most were propeller-driven, but at least two were powered by gas turbines and one racy-looking job had the appearance of a home-made rocket ship. In general the alien planes were of conventional/universal cruciform configuration, although he glimpsed at least one canard and a twin-fuselage craft.

'A bit of a mixture,' Ralston commented, and added with a note of disappointment in his voice. 'I see a lot of internal combustion engines out there. If that's the level they're at they won't be much use to us.'

'How about supplies of fossil fuel?'

'There could be some about – depends on the age of Orbitsville.' Ralston surveyed the ground below with professional disgust. 'My training isn't worth a damn out here. The ordinary rules don't apply.'

'I think it's okay to go down,' Braunek said. 'Our friend has dipped his nose a couple of times.'

'Right. Pass the word along.'

As the fringes of the alien settlement began to slide below the nose of the aircraft Braunek sat higher in his seat and turned his head rapidly from side to side. 'I can't see their airfield. We'll have to circle around.'

Garamond tapped the pilot's shoulder. 'I think you'll find they haven't got a centralized airfield.'

The aircraft banked into a turn, giving a good view of the ground. The city wheeling below the wing was at least twenty kilometres across but had no distinguishable roads, factories or other buildings larger than average-sized dwellings. Garamond's impression was of thousands of hunting lodges scattered in an area of woodland. Here and there, randomly distributed, were

154

irregular cleared areas about the size of football pitches. The brightly coloured alien planes dispersed towards these, crossing flight paths at low altitude in an uncontrolled manner which brought audible gasps from Braunek. They landed unceremoniously, one to a field, leaving the humans' ships still aloft in the circuit.

'This is crazy – I'm not going to try putting us down in somebody's back yard,' Braunek announced.

'Find a good strip outside of town and we'll land in sequence the way we'd already planned,' Garamond told him. He sat back in his seat and buckled his safety straps. The plane lost altitude, completed two low-level orbits and landed, with a short jolting run on its skids, in an expanse of meadow. Braunek steered it off to one side and they watched as the six other ships of the fleet touched down on the same tracks and formed an untidy line. Their propellers gradually stopped turning and canopies were pushed upwards like the wing casings of insects.

Green-scented air flooded in around Garamond and he relaxed for a moment, enjoying the sensation of being at rest. The luxuriousness of his body's response to the silence awakened memories of what it had been like arriving home for a brief spell after a long mission. Ecstasy-living was a phenomenon well known to S.E.A. personnel, as were its attendant dangers. Rigid self-control was always required during home leave, to prevent the ecstasy getting out of control and causing a fierce negative reaction at the beginning of the next mission. But in this instance, as he breathed the cool heavy air, Garamond realized he had been tricked into lowering his guard . . .

I can't possibly take another two years of flying night and day, the thought came. *Nobody could.*

'Come on, Vance – stretch the legs,' Braunek called as he leapt down on to the grass. He was followed in close succession by Delia Liggett, Ralston and Pierre Tarque, the young medic who completed the crew of No 1. Garamond waved to them and made himself busy with his straps.

Two whole years to go – at least ! – and what would it achieve ?

The sound of laughter and cheerful voices came from outside as the crews of the seven aircraft met and mingled. He could

155

hear friendly punches being swapped, and derisive whoops which probably signified an overlong kiss being exchanged.

Even if I get near enough to the President to kill her, which is most unlikely, what would that achieve? It's too late to do anything for Aileen and Chris. Would they want me to get myself executed?

Garamond stood up, filled with guilty excitement, and climbed out of the glasshouse. From the slight elevation, the alien settlement looked like a dreamy garden village. He glanced around, taking in all the lime-green immensities, and dropped to the ground where Cliff Napier and Denise Serra were waiting for him. Denise greeted him with a warm, direct gaze. She was wearing regulation-issue black trousers, but topped with a tangerine blouse in place of a tunic, and he suddenly appreciated that she was beautiful. They were joined almost at once by O'Hagan and Sammy Yamoto, both of whom looked greyer and older than Garamond had expected. O'Hagan wasted no time on pleasantries.

'We're at a big decision point, Vance,' he began. 'Five of our ships have sub-standard propeller bearings and if we can't get them upgraded there's no point in continuing with the flight.' He tilted his head and assumed the set expression with which he always heard arguments.

'I have to agree.' Garamond nodded, rediscovering the fact that looking at Denise produced a genuine sensation of pleasure in his eyes.

O'Hagan twitched his brows in surprise. 'All right, then. The first thing we have to do when we meet these aliens is to assess their engineering capabilities.'

'They can't be at the level of gyromagnetic power or magnetic bearings – you saw their aircraft.'

'That's true, but I think I'm right in saying a magnelube bearing can be considerably upgraded by enclosing it within another bearing, even one as primitive as a ball race. All we would have to do is commission the aliens to manufacture twenty or so large conventional bearings which we can wrap around our magnelubes.'

'They'd need to be of a standard size.'

O'Hagan sniffed loudly. 'That goes without saying.'

'I think you'll find . . .' Garamond broke off as an abrupt silence fell over the assembled crews. He turned and saw a fantastic cavalcade approaching the aircraft from the direction of the city. The aliens were humanoid – from a distance surprisingly so – and shared the human predilection for covering their bodies with clothes. Predominant hues were yellows and browns which toned in with sand-coloured skin, making it difficult to determine precise details of their anatomies. Some of the aliens were on foot, some on bicycles, some on tricycles, some on motor-cycles, some in a variety of open cars and saloons including a two-wheeled gyro car, some were perched on the outside of an erratic air-cushion vehicle. They approached to within twenty metres of the parked aircraft and came to a halt. As the heterogenous mixture of engines associated with their transport coughed, clanked and spluttered into silence, Garamond became aware that the aliens were producing a soft humming noise of their own. It was a blend of many different notes, continuously inflecting, and he tentatively concluded that it was their mode of speech. The aliens were hairless but had identifiable equivalents of eyes, ears and mouths agreeably positioned on their heads. Garamond was unable to decide what anatomical features their flimsy garments were meant to cover, or to see any evidence of sexual differentiation. He felt curiously indifferent to the aliens in spite of the fact that this first contact looked infinitely more propitious than the wordless futility of his encounter with the Clowns. No adventure in the outside universe held much significance compared to the voyage of discovery he was making within himself.

'Do you want to try speaking with them ?' O'Hagan said.

Garamond shook his head. 'It's your turn to get your name in the history books, Dennis. Be my guest.'

O'Hagan looked gratified. 'If it were done when 'tis done, then 'twere well it were done scientifically.' He advanced on the nearest of the aliens, who seemed to regard him with interest, and the movement of his shoulders showed he was trying to communicate with his hands.

'There's no *need*,' Garamond said in a low voice.

Yamoto turned his head. 'What did you say?'

'Nothing, Sammy. I was talking to myself.'

'You should be careful who you're seen speaking to.'

Garamond nodded abstractedly. *The thing Dennis O'Hagan doesn't realize about these people is that they'll never do what he wants. He has missed all the signs.*

All right – assuming we can't get them to make the bearings, is there any point in continuing with the flight? Answer: no. This isn't just a personal reaction. The computers agreed that two air-planes of the type available would not constitute a sufficiently flexible and resourceful transport system. Therefore, I simply can't get back to Beachhead City. It's as clear-cut as that. It always was too late to do anything for Aileen and Chris, and now there's nothing I can even attempt to do.

I've been born again.

*

The aliens stayed for more than an hour and then, gradually but without stragglers, moved away in the direction of their city. They reminded Garamond of children who had been enjoying an afternoon at a funfair and had become so hungry they could not bear to miss the meal waiting at home. When the last brightly painted vehicle disappeared behind the trees there was a moment of utter silence in the meadow, followed by an explosive release of tension among the plane crews. Bottles of synthetic liqueur were produced and a party set off to swim in a nearby lake.

'That was weird,' Joe Braunek said, shaking his head. 'We stood in two lines and looked at each other like farm boys and girls at a village dance on Terranova.'

'It went all right,' Garamond assured him. 'There's no pro-tocol – what are you supposed to do?'

'It still was weird.'

'I know, but just think what it would have been like if there'd been any diplomats or military around. We met them, and stared at them, and they stared at us, and nobody tried to take anything that belonged to the others, and nobody got hurt. Things could have been worse, believe me.'

'I guess so. Did you see the way they kept counting our ships?'

'I did notice that.' Garamond recalled the repeated gesture among the onlookers, long golden fingers indicating, stepping their way along the line of aircraft.

'Seemed important to them, somehow. It was as if they'd never seen . . .'

'We've made genuine progress, Vance.' O'Hagan approached with a sheaf of hand-written notes and a recorder. 'I've identified at least six nouns or noun-sounds in their speech and I believe I'd have done better if I'd had musical training.'

'Can't you get somebody to help?'

'I have. I'm taking Paskuda and Shelley and going into the city. We won't stay long.'

'Take as long as you need,' Garamond said casually.

'All right, Vance.' O'Hagan gave him a searching stare. 'I want to see something of their machine capability as soon as possible. I think that would be a good idea, don't you?'

'Excellent.' Garamond had seen a flash of tangerine further down the line of aircraft and was unable to take his eyes away from it. He quickly disengaged from O'Hagan, walked towards Denise Serra but hesitated on seeing that she was involved in a discussion with the six other women of the flight crews. He was turning away when she noticed him and signalled that he was to wait. A minute later she came to him, looking warm, competent, desirable and everything else he expected a woman to be. The thought of lying with her caused a painful stab in his lower abdomen as glandular mechanisms, too long suppressed, found themselves reactivated. Denise glanced around her, frowned at the proximity of other people, and led the way towards an un-spoiled area of tall grass. The quasi-intimacy of her actions pleased Garamond.

'It's good to see you again,' he said.

'It's good to see you, Vance. How do you feel now?'

'Better. I'm coming to life again.'

'I'm glad.' Denise gave him a speculative look. 'That was an official meeting of Orbitsville Women's League, detached chapter.'

159

'Oh? Carry on, Sister Denise.'

She smiled briefly. 'Vance, they've voted to drop out of the flight.'

'Unanimously?'

'Yes. Five airplanes are going to have to give up eventually, and we might as well pick the spot. The Hummers seem friendly and making a study of their culture will give us something to do. Apart from bringing up babies, that is.'

'Do you know how many men will want to stay?'

'Most of them. I'm sorry, Vance.'

'Nobody has to apologize for the operation of simple logic.'

'But that leaves you only two aircraft, and it isn't enough.'

'It's all right.' Garamond wondered how long he could go on with the role of martyr before telling Denise he had already come to terms with himself.

She caught his hand. 'I know how disappointed you must be.'

'You're making it easy to take,' he said. Denise released his hand on the instant and he knew he had said something wrong. He waited impassively.

'Has Cliff not told you I'm having a baby?' Denise's eyes were intent on his. 'His baby?'

Garamond forced himself to compose a suitable reply. 'He didn't need to.'

'You mean he *hasn't*? Just wait till I get my hands on the big . . .'

'I'm not completely blind, Denise.' Garamond produced a smile for her. 'I knew as soon as I saw both of you together this morning. I just haven't got around to congratulating him yet.'

'Thanks, Vance. Out here we'll need all the godfathers we can get.'

'Can't help you there, I'm afraid – I'll be a few million kilometres east of here by that time.'

'Oh!' Denise looked away from him. 'I thought . . .'

'That I was quitting? Not until I'm forced – and you know better than I do that the computers didn't say two aircraft *couldn't* reach Beachhead City. It's just a question of odds, isn't it?'

'So is Russian Roulette.'

'I'll see you around, Denise.' Garamond turned away, but she caught his arm.

'I shouldn't have said that. I'm sorry.'

'Please forget it.' He squeezed her hand before removing it from his arm. 'I really am glad that you and Cliff have got something good. Now, please excuse me – I have a lot of work to do.'

*

Garamond had been occupied for several hours on the load distribution plans for his two remaining aircraft when darkness came. He switched on the fuselage interior lights and continued working with cold concentration, ignoring the sounds of revelry which drifted into the cabin on the evening breeze. His fingers moved continually over the calculator keyboard as he laboured through dozens of load permutations, striving to decide the best uses for his payload capability. The brief penumbral twilight had fled when he felt vibrations which told him someone was coming on board. He looked up and saw O'Hagan squeezing his way towards the small chart-covered table.

'I've just discovered how much I used to rely on computers,' Garamond said.

O'Hagan shook his head impatiently. 'I've just spent the most fantastic day of my life, and I need a drink to get over it. Where's the supply?' He sat quietly while Garamond found a plastic bottle and handed it to him, then he took a short careful swallow. 'This stuff hasn't been aged much.'

'The man who made it has.'

'Like the rest of us.' O'Hagan took another drink and apparently decided he had devoted too much time to preamble. 'We haven't got a hope in hell of getting the bearings we need from these people. Know why?'

'Because they've no machine tools?'

'Because they make everything by hand. You knew?'

'I guessed. They've got some airplanes, but no airplane factory or airport. They've got some cars, but no car factory or roads.'

'Good work, Vance – you were way ahead on that one.'

O'Hagan drummed his fingers on the table, the sound filling the narrow confines of the cabin, and his voice lost some of its usual incisiveness. 'They picked an entirely different road to ours. No specialization of labour, no mass production, no standardization. Anybody who wants a car or a cake-mixer builds it from scratch, if he has the time and the talent. You noticed their planes and cars were all different?'

'Yes. I noticed them counting our ships, too.'

'So did I, but I didn't know what was going on in their minds. They must have been astonished at seeing seven identical models.'

'Not astonished,' Garamond said. 'Mildly surprised, perhaps. I've a feeling these people haven't much curiosity in their make-up. If you allow only one alien per house that city out there must have a population of twenty thousand or more, but I doubt if as many as two hundred came out to look at us today – and practically all those who came had their own transport.'

'You mean we got the lunatic fringe.'

'Gadgeteers anyway – probably more interested in our aircraft than in us. They could be a frustrating bunch to have as next door neighbours.'

O'Hagan stared significantly at the paperwork scattered on the table. 'So you intend to press on?'

'Yes.' Garamond decided to let the single word do the work of the hundreds he might have used.

'Have you got a crew?'

'I don't know yet.'

O'Hagan sighed heavily. 'I'm sick to death of flying, Vance. It's killing me. But I'd go crazy if I had to live beside somebody who kept inventing the steam engine every couple of years. I'll fly with you.'

'Thanks, Dennis.' Garamond felt a warm prickling in his eyes. 'I . . .'

'Never mind the gratitude,' O'Hagan said briskly. 'Let's see what sort of mess you've been making of these load distributions.'

*

Against Garamond's expectations, he was able to raise two crews of four to continue the flight. Again making use of the extra lift to be gained from cold air, the two machines took off at dawn and, without circling or giving any aerial signal of goodbye, they flew quietly into the east.

eighteen

Day 193. Estimated range: 2,160,000 kilometres

This may be my last journal entry. Words seem to be losing their meaning, the act of writing them is losing all significance, and I notice that we have virtually stopped speaking to each other. The silence does not imply or induce separateness – the eight of us have compacted into one. It is simply that there is something embarrassing about watching a man go through the whole pointless performance of shaping his lips and activating his tongue in order to push sound vibrations out on the air. It is peculiar, too, how a spoken word resolves itself into meaningless syllables, and how a single syllable can hang resonating in the air, in your mind, long after the speaker has turned away.

I fancy, sometimes, that the same phenomenon takes place with images. We have steered our ships above a thousand seas, ten thousand mountain ranges, all of which have promised to be different – but which are all becoming the same. A distinctive peak or river bend, a curious group of islands, the coloration of a wooded valley – geographical features appear before us with the promise of something new and, having cheated us, fall behind. Were it not for the certainty of the inertial guidance system I might imagine we were flying in circles. No, that isn't correct, for we have learned to steer a constant course against the stripings of the sky. We seem to exist, embedded, in a huge crystal paperweight and one of the advantages, perhaps the only one, is that we can tell where we are going by reference to its millefiori design. If I hold the milk-blue curvatures in a certain precise relationship, crossing windshield and prow just so, I can fly for as long as thirty minutes before the black box chimes and edges me to left or right. The other black box, the portable delton detector, remains inert even after all this time. (Dennis was right when he said we were lucky to find that first particle so soon.) The up-curving horizon provides a constant reference for level flying. It occurred to me recently that Orbitsville is so big that we should not be able to detect any upward curvature in the horizon. As usual, Dennis was able to explain that it was an optical illusion – the horizon is straight but, through a trick of perception, appears to sag in the middle. He told me that the ancient Greeks compensated for this when building their temples.

The two aircraft are behaving as well as can be expected within their design limits. Each is carrying a reserve power-plant which takes up a high proportion of its payload, but this is unavoidable. A gyromagnetic engine is little more than a block of metal in which most of the atoms have been orchestrated to resonate in tune. It is without doubt one of the best general-purpose medium-sized power-plants ever conceived, but it has a fault in that – without warning and for no apparent reason – the orchestra can fall into discord and the power output drops to zero. When that happens there is no option than to install a new engine, so we can afford it to happen only twice. We have also had minor mechanical troubles. As yet there has been nothing serious enough to cause an unscheduled landing, but the potential is always there and grows daily.

The biggest cause for concern, however, is the biological machinery on board – our own bodies. Everybody, except for young Braunek, is subject to headaches, constipation, dizziness and nausea. Many of the symptoms are probably due to pro-longed stress but, with increasingly unreliable aircraft to fly, we dare not resort to tranquillizers. Dennis, in particular, is causing me alarm and an equal amount of guilt over having brought him along. He gets greyer and more tired every day, and less and less able to do his stint at the controls. The protein and yeast cakes on which we live are not appetizing at the best of times, but Dennis is finding it almost impossible to keep them down and his weight is decreasing rapidly.

I am reaching the conclusion that the mission should be abandoned, and this time there are no emotional undertones in my thinking. I know it is not worth the expenditure of human lives.

A short time ago I could not have made such an admission – but that was before we had fully begun to pay for our mistake of challenging the Big O. The journey we attempted was perhaps only a hundredth of O's circumference, and of that tiny fraction we have completed only a fraction. My personal punishment for this presumption is that O has scoured out my soul. I can think of my dead wife and child; I can think of Denise Serra; I can think of Elizabeth Lindstrom . . . and nothing happens.

I feel nothing.

This is my last diary entry.

There is nothing more to write.

There is nothing more to say.

*

Kneeling on the thrumming floor beside O'Hagan's bunk, Garamond said, 'It's summertime down there, Dennis. We've flown right into summer.'

'I don't care.' Beneath its covering of sheets, the scientist's body seemed as frail and fleshless as that of a mummified woman.

'I'm positive we could find fruit trees.'

O'Hagan gave a skeletal grin. 'You know what you can do with your fruit trees.'

'But if you could eat something you'd be all right.'

'I'm just fine – all I need is a rest.' O'Hagan caught Garamond's wrist. 'Vance, you're not going to call off the flight on my account. Promise me that.'

'I promise.' Garamond disengaged the white, too-clean fingers one by one and stood up. The decision, now that it had come, was strangely easy to make. 'I'm calling it off on my own account.'

He ignored the other man's protests and went forward along

the narrow aisle to the blinding arena of the cockpit. Braunke was at the controls and Sammy Yamoto was beside him in the second pilot's seat. He had removed a cover from the delton detector and was probing inside it. Garamond tapped him on the shoulder.

'Why aren't you asleep, Sammy? You were on duty most of the night.'

Yamoto adjusted his dark glasses. 'I'm going to kip down in a minute – as soon as I put my mind at rest about this pile of junk.'

'Junk?'

'Yes. I don't think it's working.'

Garamond glanced at the detector's control panel. 'According to the operating light it's working.'

'I know, but look at this.' Yamoto clicked the switch of the main power supply to the detector box up and down several times in succession. The orange letters which spelled, SYSTEM FUNCTIONING, continued to glow steadily in their dark recess.

'What a botch,' Yamoto said bitterly. 'You know, I might never have caught on if a generator hadn't cut itself out during the night. I was sitting here about two hours later when, all of a sudden, it hit me – the lights on the detector panel hadn't blinked with all the others.'

'Does that prove it isn't working?'

'Not necessarily – but it makes me doubt the quality of the whole assembly. Litman deserves to be shot.'

'Don't worry about it.' Garamond lowered himself into the supernumerary seat. 'Not at this stage anyway – we have to call off the flight.'

'Dennis?'

'Yes. It's killing him.'

'I don't want to seem callous, but . . .' Yamoto paused to force a multi-connector into place, '. . . don't you think he could die anyway?'

'I can't take that chance.'

'Now I *have* to sound callous. There are seven other men on this . . .' Yamoto stopped speaking as the delton detector emitted a sharp tap, like a steel ball dropped on to a metal plate. He instinctively jerked his hand away from the exposed wiring.

Garamond raised his eyebrows. 'What have you done to it?'

'All I've done is fix it.' Yamoto gave a quivering, triumphant grin as two more tapping sounds were heard almost simultaneously.

'Then what are those noises?'

'Those, my friend, are delta particles going through our screen.' The astronomer's words were punctuated by further noises from the machine. 'And their frequency indicates that we are close to their source.'

'Close? How close?'

Yamoto took out a calculator and his fingers flickered over it. 'I'd say about twenty or thirty thousand kilometres.'

A cool breeze from nowhere played on Garamond's forehead. 'You don't mean from Beachhead City.'

'Beachhead City is the only source we know. That's what it's all about.'

'But . . .' A fresh staccato outburst came from the detector as Garamond, knowing he should have been excited, looked out through the front windshield of the aircraft at a range of low mountains perhaps an hour's flying time ahead. They seemed no more and no less familiar than all the others he had seen.

'Is this possible?' he said. 'Could we have overestimated the flight time by two years?'

Yamoto turned an adjusting screw on the delton detector, decreasing the sound level of its irregular tattoo. 'Anything is possible on Orbitsville.'

*

It was late on the following day when the two stiff-winged, ungainly birds began to gain altitude to cross the final green ridges. All crew members, including a fever-eyed O'Hagan, were gathered to watch as the mountain crests began to sink in submission to their combined wills. Changing parallaxes made the high ground below them appear to shift like sand.

Yamoto switched off the detector's incessant roar with a flourish. 'The instrument is no longer of any use to us. Astronomically speaking, we have reached our destination.'

'How far would you say it is, Sammy?'

'A hundred kilometres. Perhaps less.'

Joe Braunek squirmed in his seat, but his hands and feet were steady on the flying controls. 'Then we have to see Beachhead City as soon as we clear this range.'

Garamond felt the conviction which had been growing in him achieve a leaden solidity. 'It won't be there,' he announced. 'I don't remember seeing a mountain range this close to the city.'

'It's a pretty low range,' Yamoto said uncertainly. 'You wouldn't have noticed it unless you had a specific . . .'

His voice faded as the ground tilted and sloped away beneath them to reveal one of Orbitsville's mind-stilling prairies. In the hard clean light of the sun they could see to the edges of infinity, across oceans of grass and scrub, and there was no sign of Beachhead City.

'What do we do now?' Braunek spoke with a curious timidity as he looked back at the other three men. The resilience which all the months of flight had not been able to sap now seemed to have left him. 'Do we just fly on?'

Garamond, unable to feel shock or disappointment, turned to Yamoto. 'Switch the detector on again.'

'Right.' The astronomer reactivated the black box and the cabin immediately filled with its roar. 'But we can't change what it says – we're right on target.'

'Is it directional?'

'Yes.' Yamoto glanced at O'Hagan, who nodded tiredly in confirmation.

'Swing to the left,' Garamond told Braunek. 'Not too quickly.' The plane banked slowly to the north and, as it did so, the sound from the delton detector steadily decreased until it faded out altogether.

'Hold it there! We're now flying at right angles to the precise source of the particle bombardment. Right, Sammy?'

Yamoto raised the binoculars and looked in the direction indicated by the aircraft's starboard wing. 'It's no use, Vance. There's nothing there.'

'There has to be something. We've got an hour of daylight left – take a new bearing and we'll follow it till nightfall.'

While Yamoto used the lightphone to bring the second crew up to date on what was happening, Joe Braunek steered the aircraft on to its new heading and shed height until they were at cruise altitude. The two machines flew onwards for another hour, occasionally swinging off course to make an up-dated check on their direction. Towards the end of the hour O'Hagan's strength gave out and he had to be helped back to his bunk.

'We messed it up,' he said to Garamond, easing himself down.

Garamond shook his head as he covered the older man's thin body. 'It wasn't your fault.'

'Our basic premise was wrong, and that's unforgivable.'

'Forget it, Dennis. Besides, you were the one who warned me we had no right to pick up that first particle so soon. As usual, you were right.'

'Don't try to butter me. I'm too . . .' O'Hagan closed his eyes and seemed to fall asleep at once. Garamond made his way back to the cockpit and sat down to weigh up the various factors involved in the ending of the mission. He sensed that the resistance of the other men, which had surprised him earlier, would no longer be a consideration. They had allowed themselves to hope too soon, and Orbitsville had punished them for it. What remained now was the decision on where to make the final landing. His own preference was for the foothills of a mountain chain which would provide them with rivers, variety of vegetation and the psychologically important richness of scenery. It might be best to turn back to the range they had just crossed rather than fly onwards over what seemed to be the greatest plain they had encountered so far. There was the possibility that something could go wrong with one of the aircraft when they were part way across that eternity of grass; and there was the certainty that what they would find on the far side would be no different to what they had left behind. Unless they came to a sea, Garamond reminded himself. A sea would add even more . . .

'I think we've arrived,' Braunek called over his shoulder. 'I see something in front of us.'

Garamond moved up behind the pilot and peered through the forward canopy at the flat prairie. It stretched ahead, unbroken, for hundreds of kilometres. 'I don't see anything,' he said.

'Straight ahead of us. About ten kilometres.'

'Is it something small?'

'Small? It's huge! Look, Vance, right there!'

Garamond followed the exact line of Braunek's pointing finger and a cold unease crept over him as he confirmed his belief that they were looking at featureless flatlands.

Yamoto shouldered his way into the cockpit. 'What's going on?'

'Straight ahead of us,' Braunek said. 'What do you think that is?'

The astronomer shielded his eyes to see better and gave a low whistle. 'I don't know, but it would be worth landing for a closer look. But before we go down I want to get an infrared photograph of it.'

Garamond examined the sand-smooth plain once more, and was opening his mouth to protest when he saw the apparition. He had been looking for an object which distinguished itself from its surroundings by verticality and texture, but this was a vast area of grass which differed from the rest only in that it was slightly darker in colour. It could have been taken for a natural variation in the grass, perhaps caused by soil composition, except for the fact that it was perfectly circular. From the approaching aircraft it appeared as a ghostly ellipse of green on green, like a design in an experimental painting. Yamoto opened his personal locker, took out a camera and photographed the slowly expanding circle. He reeled the print out, glanced at it briefly and passed it round for the others to see. On it the area of grass stood out darkly against an orange background.

'It's quite a few degrees colder,' Yamoto said. 'I would say that the entire area seems to be losing heat into space.'

'What does it mean?'

'Well, the grass there is of a slightly different colour to the rest – which could mean the soil is absorbing some mineral or other. And there's the heat loss. *Plus* the fact that radiation from the outside universe is being admitted . . . It adds up to just one thing.'

'Which is?'

'We've found another entrance to Orbitsville.'

'How can that be?' Garamond felt a slow unexpected quickening of his spirit. 'We did a survey of the equatorial region from the outside, and besides . . . there's no hole in the shell.'

'There is a hole,' Yamoto said calmly. 'But – a very long time ago – somebody sealed it up.'

*

They landed close to the edge of the circle and, although darkness came flooding in from the east only a few minutes later, began to dig an exploratory trench. The soil was several metres thick in the area, but in less than an hour an invisible resistance to their spades told them they had encountered the lenticular field. A short time later a massive diaphragm of rusting metal was uncovered. They sliced through it with the invisible lance of a valency cutter.

Two men levered a square section upwards and then, without speaking the others took it in turn to look downwards at the stars.

nineteen

'This is North Ten, the most advanced of our forward distribution centres,' Elizabeth Lindstrom said, with a warm note of pride in her voice. 'You can see at once the amount of effort and organization that has been put into it.'

Charles Devereaux walked across to the parapet of the roof of the administration building and looked out across the plain. Four hundred kilometres to the south lay Beachhead City, and the arrow-straight highway to it was alive with the small wheeled transports of settlers. Here and there on the road, before it faded into the shimmering distance, could be seen the larger shapes of bulk carriers bringing supplies. The highway ended at North Ten, from which point a series of dirt tracks fanned out into the encircling sweep of prairie. For the first few kilometres the tracks made their way through an industrial area where reaping machines gathered the grass which was used as a source of cellulose to produce plastics for building purposes. Immediately beyond the acetate factories the homesteads began, with widely spaced buildings sparkling whitely in the sun.

'I'm impressed with everything Starflight has done here, My Lady,' Devereaux said, choosing his words with professional care. 'Please understand that when I put questions to you I do so solely in my capacity as a representative of the Two Worlds Government.'

Do you think I would waste time answering them otherwise? Elizabeth suppressed the thought and bent her mind to the unfamiliar task of self-control. 'I do understand,' she assured the dapper grey man, smiling. 'It's your duty to make sure that all that can possibly be done to open up Lindstromland is in fact being done.'

'That's precisely it, My Lady. You see, the people on Earth and Terranova have heard about the fantastic size of Lindstromland and they can't understand why it is that, if there is unlimited living space available, the Government doesn't simply set up a programme of shipbuilding on a global scale and bring them here.'

'A perfectly understandable point of view, but . . .' Elizabeth spread her hands to the horizons, fingers flashing with jewel-fire, '. . . this land I have given to humanity makes its own rules and we have no option but to abide by them. Lindstromland is unthinkably large, but by providing only one entrance – and placing restrictions on interior travel and communications – its builders have effectively made it small. My own belief is that they decided to enforce a selection procedure, or its equivalent. As long as Lindstromland can accept immigrants only in regulated quantities the quality of the stock which arrives will be higher.'

'Do you think the concept of stock and breeding would have been familiar to them?'

'Perhaps not.' Elizabeth realized she had used an unfortunate trigger-word, one to which the upstart of a civil servant reacted unfavourably. It struck her that things had already gone too far when she, President of Starflight, was being forced to placate an obscure official in the weakest government in human history. The circumstances surrounding the discovery of Lindstromland, she was beginning to appreciate, had been ill omens.

Devereaux apparently was not satisfied. 'It would be a tragedy if Earth were to export attitudes such as nationalism and . . .'

'What I'm saying,' Elizabeth cut in, 'is that it would be an even bigger tragedy if we were to empty every slum and gutter on Earth into this green land.'

'Why?' Devereaux met her eyes squarely and she made the discovery that his greyness had a steely quality. 'Because the transportation task would be too great to be handled by a private concern?'

Elizabeth felt her mouth go dry as she fought to restrain herself. Nobody had ever been allowed to speak to her in this manner before, with the possible exception of Captain Garamond – and he had paid. It was infuriating how these small men, nonentities, tended to lapse into insolence the moment they felt secure.

'Of course not,' she said, marvelling at the calmness of her voice. 'There are many sound reasons for regulating population flow. Look at the squalid difficulties there were when the first settlers here encountered those creatures they call Clowns.'

'Yes, but those difficulties could have been avoided. In fact, we think they may have been engineered.'

For one heady moment Elizabeth considered burning Devereaux in two where he stood, even if it led to a major incident, even if it meant turning Lindstromland into a fortress. Then it came to her that Devereaux – in abandoning all the rules of normal diplomacy – was laying his cards on the table. She regarded him closely for a moment, trying to decide if he was offering himself for sale. The approach, in greatly modified form, was a familiar one among government employees – show yourself to be dangerous and therefore valuable in proportion. She smiled and moved closer to Devereaux, deliberately stepping inside his proximity rejection zone, a psychological manoeuvre she had learned at an early age. His face stiffened momentarily, as she had known it would, and she was about to touch him when Secretary Robard appeared on the edge of the stair-well. He was carrying a headset and feeding wire out of a reel as he walked.

Elizabeth frowned at him. 'What is this, Robard?'

'Priority One, My Lady. Your flagship is picking up a radio message which you must hear.'

'Wait there.' She moved away from Devereaux. The brusqueness of her man's voice, so out of keeping with his normal manner, told her something important had happened. She silently cursed the obtuse physics of Lindstromland which had denied her easy radio contact with the outside universe. A voice was already speaking when she put on the headset. It was unemotional, with an inhuman steadiness, and the recognition of it drained the strength from her legs. Elizabeth Lindstrom sank to her knees, and listened.

'. . . using the resources of the *Bissendorf*'s workshops we built a number of aircraft with which it was planned to fly back to Beachhead City. The ships proved inadequate for the distance involved, but they got eight of us to the point from which I am making this broadcast, the point where we have discovered a second entrance to the sphere.

'The entrance was not discovered during the equatorial survey because it is sealed with a metal diaphragm. The metal employed has nothing in common with the material of the Orbitsville shell. I believe it is the product of a civilization no further advanced than our own. This belief is strengthened by the fact that we had no difficulty in cutting a hole in it to let us extend a radio antenna.'

There was a crackling pause, then the voice emerged strongly in its relentless measured tones. 'The fact that we were able to find a second entrance so quickly, with such limited resources, can only mean that there must be many others. Many hundreds. Many thousands. It is logical to assume that all the others have been similarly blocked, and it is equally logical to assume that it was not done by the builders of the sphere.

'This raises questions about the identity and motivation of those who sealed the entrances. The evidence suggests that the work was carried out by a race of beings who found Orbitsville long before we did. We may never know what these beings looked like, but we can tell that they shared some of the faults of our own race. They, or some of them, decided to monopolize Orbitsville, to control it, to exploit it; and the method they chose was to limit access to the interior of the sphere.

'The evidence also shows that they succeeded – and that, eventually, they failed.

'Perhaps they were destroyed in the battle we know to have taken place at the Beachhead City entrance. Perhaps in the end they lost out to Orbitsville itself. By being absorbed and changed, just as we are going to be absorbed and changed. The lesson for us now is that the entire Starflight organization – with its vested interest in curbing humanity's natural expansion – must be set aside. All of Orbitsville is open to us. It is available as I speak...'

Elizabeth removed the headset, cutting herself off from the dreadful didactic voice. She put her hands on the smooth surface of the roof and sank down until she was lying prone, her open mouth pressed against the foot-printed plastic.

Vance Garamond, she thought, her mind sinking through successive levels of cryogenic coldness. *I have to love you . . . because you are the only one ever to have given me real pain, ever to hurt me, and hurt me.* She moved her hips from side to side, grinding against the roof with her pubis. *Now that all else is ending . . . it is my turn . . . to make love . . . to you . . .*

'My Lady, are you ill?' The voice reached her across bleak infinities. Elizabeth raised her head and, with effort, identified the grey anxious face of Charles Devereaux. She got to her feet.

'How dare you!' she said coldly. 'What are you suggesting?'

'Nothing. I . . .'

'Why did you let this . . . *object* enter my quarters?' Elizabeth turned and stared accusingly at Robard who had quietly retrieved the headset and was reeling in the attached wire. 'Get him out of here!'

'I'm going – I've seen enough.' Devereaux hurried towards the stairwell. Elizabeth watched him go, twisting a ruby ring on her finger as she did so. It turned easily on bearings of perspiration.

Robard bowed nervously. 'If you will excuse me . . .'

'Not yet,' Elizabeth snapped. 'Get me Doctor Killops on that thing.'

175

'Yes, My Lady.' Robard murmured into the instrument, listened for a moment, and then handed it to her. He began to withdraw but she pointed at a spot nearby, silently ordering him to stay.

Elizabeth raised the communicator to her lips. 'Tell me, Doctor Killops, has Mrs Garamond had her sedative today yet? No? Then don't give it to her. Captain Garamond is returning, alive, and we want his wife to be fully conscious and alert for the reunion.' She threw the instrument down and Robard stooped to pick it up.

'Never mind that,' Elizabeth said quietly. 'Get my car ready to leave in five minutes. I have urgent business in Beachhead City.'

*

The shock of hearing by radio that his wife and son were still alive had stormed through Garamond's system like a nuclear fireball. In its wake had come relief, joy, gratitude, bafflement, renewal of optimism – and finally, as a consequence of emotional overload, an intense physical reaction. There was a period of several hours during which he experienced cold sweats, irregular heartbeat and dizziness; and the symptoms were at their height when the little transit boat from fleet headquarters arrived underfoot.

As had happened once before, he felt disoriented and afraid on seeing a spacesuited figure clamber upwards through a black hole in the ground. The figure was followed by others who were carrying empty spacesuits, and – even when the faceplates had been removed and the two parties were mingling – they still looked strange to him. At some time in the preceding months he had come to accept the thin-shouldered shabbiness of his own crew as the norm, and now the members of the rescue party seemed too sleek and shiny, too alien.

'Captain Garamond?' A youthful Starflight officer approached him and saluted, beardless face glowing with pleasure and health. 'I'm Lieutenant Kenny of the *Westmorland*. This is a great honour for me, sir.'

'Thank you.' The action of returning the salute felt awkward to Garamond.

Kenny's gaze strayed to the sloping, stiff-winged outlines of the two aircraft and his jaw sagged. 'I'm told you managed to fly a couple of million kilometres in those makeshifts. That must have been *fantastic*.'

Garamond suppressed an illogical resentment. 'You might call it that. The *Westmorland*? Isn't that Hugo Schilling's command?'

'Captain Schilling insisted on coming with us. He's waiting for you aboard the transit boat now. I'll have to photograph those airplanes, sir – they're just too . . .'

'Not now, Lieutenant. My Chief Science Officer is very ill and he must be hospitalized at once. The rest of us aren't in great shape, either.' Garamond tried to keep his voice firm even though a numbness had enveloped his body, creating a sensation that his head was floating in the air like a balloon.

Kenny, with a flexibility of response which further dismayed Garamond, was instantly solicitous. He began shouting orders and within a few minutes the eight members of the *Bissendorf*'s crew had been suited up for transfer to the waiting boat. Garamond's mind was brimming with thoughts of Aileen and Chris as he negotiated the short spacewalk, with its swaying vistas of star rivers and its constrained breathing of rubber-smelling air. As soon as he had passed through the airlock he made his way to the forward compartment, which seemed impossibly roomy after his months in the aircraft's narrow fuselage. Another spacesuited figure rose to greet him.

'It's good to see you, Vance,' Hugo Schilling said. He was a blue-eyed, silver-haired man who had been in the Exploration Arm for twenty years and treated his job of wandering unknown space as if he was the pilot of a local ferry.

'Thanks, Hugo. It's good to . . .' Garamond shook his head to show he had run out of words.

Schilling inspected him severely. 'You don't look well, Vance. Rough trip?'

'Rough trip.'

'Enough said, skipper. We're keeping the suits on, but strap yourself in and relax – we'll have you home in no time. Try to get some sleep.'

Garamond nodded gratefully. 'Have you seen my wife and boy?'

'No. Unlike you, I'm just a working flickerwing man and I don't get invited out to the Octagon.'

'The Octagon! What are they doing out there?'

'They've been staying with the President ever since you . . . ah . . . disappeared. They're celebrities too, you know – even if there is some reflection of glory involved.'

'But . . .' A new centre of coldness began to form within Garamond's body. 'Tell me, Hugo, did the President send you out here to pick us up?'

'No. It was an automatic reaction on the part of Fleet Command. The President is out at North Ten – that's one of the forward supply depots we've built.'

'Will she have heard my first message yet?'

'Probably,' Schilling pointed a gloved finger at Garamond. 'Starting to sweat over some of those things you said about Starflight? Don't worry about it – we all know you've been under a strain. You can say you got a bit carried away with the sense of occasion.'

Garamond took a deep breath. 'Are there any airplanes or other rapid transport systems in use around Beachhead City?'

'Not yet. All the production has been concentrated on ground cars and housing.'

'How long will it take the President to get back to the Octagon?'

'It's hard to say – the cars they produce aren't built for speed. Eight hours, maybe.'

'How long till we get back?'

'Well, I'm allowing five hours in view of Mister O'Hagan's condition.'

'Speed it up, Hugo,' Garamond said. 'I have to be back before the President, and she's had a few hours' start.'

Schilling glanced at the information panel on which changing colour configurations showed that the ship was sealed and almost ready for flight. 'That would mean fairly high G-forces. For a sick man . . .'

'He won't mind – go ask him.'

'I don't see . . .'

'Supposing I said it was a matter of life or death?'

'I wouldn't believe you, but . . .' Schilling winked reassuringly, opened an audio channel to the flight deck and instructed the pilot to make the return journey in the shortest possible time consistent with O'Hagan's health. Garamond thanked him and tried to relax into the G-chair, wishing he had been able to take the other man into his confidence. Schilling was kindly and un-complicated, with a high regard for authority. It would have been difficult, possibly disastrous, for Garamond to try telling him he believed Elizabeth Lindstrom was a psychopath who would enjoy murdering an innocent woman and child. Schilling might counter by asking why Elizabeth had not done it as soon as she had had the chance, and Garamond would not have been able to answer. It would not have been enough to say that he felt it in his bones. He closed his eyes as the acceleration forces clamped down, but his growing conviction of danger made it impossible for him to rest. Thirty minutes into the flight he got an idea.

'Do you think there'll be a reception when we get back? A public one?'

'Bound to be,' Schilling said. 'You keep hogging the news. Even while you were away a reporter called Mason, I think, ran a campaign to persuade somebody to go looking for your ship. The betting was fifty-to-one you were dead, though, so he didn't have much success.'

Garamond had forgotten about the reporter from Earth. 'You said my wife and boy are well known, too. I want them to meet me at the Beachhead City transit tube. Can you arrange that?'

'I don't see why not – there's a direct communications link to the Octagon from the President's flagship.' Schilling spoke into the command microphone of his spacesuit, waited, spoke again, and then settled into a lengthy conversation. Only occa-sional whispers of sound came through his open faceplate, but Garamond could hear the exchange becoming heated. When it had finished Schilling sat perfectly still for a moment before turning to speak.

'Sorry, Vance.'

'What happened?'

'Apparently the President has sent instructions from North Ten that your family are to wait in the Octagon until you get there. She's on her way there now, and they can't contact her, so nobody would authorize transportation into the City for your wife. I don't understand it.'

'I think I do,' Garamond replied quietly, his eyes fixed on the forward view plate and its image of a universe which was divided in two by the cosmic hugeness of Orbitsville, one half in light, the other in total darkness.

*

The effort of moving under multiple gravities was almost too much for Garamond, but he was standing in the cramped airlock – sealed up and breathing suit air – before the transit boat reached the docking clamps. He cracked the outer seal on the instant the green disembarkation light came on, went through the boat's outer door and found himself in a lighted L-shaped tube. It was equipped with handrails and at the rounded corner, where the sphere's gravitation came into effect, there was the beginning of a non-skid walkway.

Garamond pulled himself along the weightless section with his hands, forced his way through the invisible syrup of the lenticular field, achieved an upright position and strode into the arrival hall. He was immediately walled in by faces and bodies and, as soon as he had opened his helmet, battered by the sound of shouting and cheering. People surged around him, reaching for his hands, slapping his back, pulling hoses and connectors from his suit for souvenirs.

At the rear of the crowd were men with scene recorders and, as he scanned their faces, an uncontrollable impulse caused Garamond to raise his arm like a Twentieth Century astronaut returning from an orbital mission. He cursed the autonomous limb, appalled at its behaviour, and concentrated on finding the right face in the bewildering seething mass, aware of how much he had always depended on Cliff Napier in similar circumstances. There was a high proportion of men in the uniforms of top-ranking Starflight officials, any of whom could have arranged transport to the Octagon, but he had no way of knowing which were members of Elizabeth's inner cadre and therefore hostile. After a blurred moment he saw a heavy-shouldered young man with prematurely greying hair working his way towards him and recognized Colbert Mason. He caught the outstretched hand between both of his gloves.

'Captain Garamond,' Mason shouted above the background noise, 'I can't tell you how much . . .'

Garamond shook his head. 'We'll talk later. Have you a car?'

'It's outside.'

'I've got to get out of here right now.'

Mason hesitated. 'There's official Starflight transportation laid on.'

'Remember the first day we met, Colbert? You needed wheels in a hurry and I . . .'

'Come on.' Mason lowered his head and went through the crowd like an ice-breaking ship with Garamond, hampered by the bulk of the suit, struggling in his wake. In a matter of seconds they had reached a white vehicle which had 'TWO WORLDS NEWS AGENCY' blazoned on its side in orange letters. The two men got in, watched by the retinue which had followed them from the hall, and Mason got the vehicle moving.

'Where to?' he said.

'The Octagon – as fast as this thing will go.'

'Okay, but I'm not welcome out there. The guards won't let this car in.'

'I'm not welcome either, but we're going in just the same.' Garamond began working on the zips of the spacesuit.

That was a good line to hand the Press, he thought as the yammerings of panic began to build up. *That was an authentic general-purpose man of action speaking. Why do I do these things? Why don't I let him know I'm scared shitless? It might make things easier . . .*

Mason hunched over the wheel as he sped them through the industrial environs of the city. 'This is the part you flattened, but they rebuilt it just as ugly as ever.'

'They would.'

'Can you tell me what's going on?'

Garamond hesitated. 'Sorry, Colbert – not yet.'

'I just wondered.'

'Either way, you're going to get another big story.'

'Hell, I know that much already. I just wondered . . . as a friend.'

'I appreciate the friendship, but I can't talk till I'm sure.'

'It's all right,' Mason said. 'We'll be there in less than ten minutes.'

For the rest of the short drive Garamond concentrated on removing the spacesuit. In the confines of the car it was an exhausting, frustrating task which he welcomed because it enabled his mind to hold back the tides of fear. By the time he had finally worked himself free the octagonal building which housed the Starflight Centre was looming on a hilltop straight ahead, and he could see the perimeter fence with its strolling guards. As the car gained height, and greater stretches of the surrounding grasslands came into view, Garamond saw that there was also a northern approach road to the Octagon. Another vehicle, still several kilometres away, was speeding down it, trailing a plume of saffron dust. It was too far away for him to distinguish the black-and-silver Starflight livery, but on the instant a steel band seemed to clamp around his chest, denying him air. He stared wordlessly at the massive gate of the west entrance which was beginning to fill the car's windshield. The car slowed down as guards emerged from their kiosk.

'Go straight through it,' Garamond urged. 'Don't slow down.'

'It's no use,' Mason said. 'It would take a tank to batter down that gate – we'd both be killed. We'll just have to talk our way in.'

'*Talk?*' Garamond looked north and saw that the other vehicle seemed to be approaching with the speed of an aircraft. 'There's no time for talking.'

He leaped from the car as soon as it had slid to a halt and ran to the kiosk at the side of the gate. A sunvisored guard emerged, carrying a rifle, and stared warily at Garamond's stained travesty of a Starflight uniform.

'State your business,' he said, at the same time making a signal to the other two guards who were seated inside.

'I'm Captain Garamond of the Stellar Exploration Arm. Open the gate immediately.'

'I don't know if I can do that, Captain.'

'You've heard of me, haven't you? You know who I am?'

'I know who you are, Captain, but that doesn't mean I should let you in. Have you an authorization?'

'Authorization?' Garamond considered putting on a display of righteous indignation, but decided it would not work coming from a man who looked like a hobo. He smiled and pointed at the dust-devil which was now within a kilometre of the northern gate. 'There's my authorization. President Lindstrom is in that car, coming here specially to meet me.'

'How do I know that's true?'

'You'll know when she finds out you wouldn't let me through. I think I'll go back to my car and watch what happens.' Garamond turned away.

'Just a minute.' The guard gave Garamond a perplexed look. 'You can come in, but that other guy stays where he is.'

Garamond shrugged and walked straight at the gate. It rolled out of his way just in time, then he was inside the perimeter and heading for the Octagon's west entrance door, not more than a hundred paces away. A second before it was lost to view behind the flank of the building, he glimpsed the other car arriving at the north gate. It was black and silver, and he was able to see a pale feminine figure in the shaded interior. The certainty of being too late made his heart lapse into an unsteady, lumping rhythm. He was breaking into a run, regardless of what the watchful patrolmen might think, when his attention was caught by a flicker of movement as a window opened in the transparent wall of the uppermost floor. Again he picked out a womanly figure, but this time it was that of his wife. And she was looking down at him.

He cupped his hands to his mouth and shouted. '*Aileen!* Can you hear me?'

'*Vance!*' Her voice was faint and tremulous, almost lost in the updraft at the sheer wall.

'Pick up Christopher and bring him down to this door as fast as you can.' He indicated the nearby entrance. 'Did you get that?'

'Yes – I'm coming down.'

Aileen vanished from the window. Garamond went to the door, held it open and saw a short deserted corridor with four openings on each side. He debated trying to find stairs or elevator shaft, then decided that if he tried to meet Aileen part way he might miss her. Elizabeth was bound to be in the building by this time and on her way up to the private suite. Aileen and Christopher should be on their way down – but supposing there was only one central stairwell and they met Elizabeth head on? Garamond entered a chill dimension of time in which entire galaxies were created and destroyed between each thunderous beat of his heart. He tried to think constructively, but all that was left to him was the ability to be afraid, to feel pain and terror and . . .

One of the corridor doors burst open. He caught a flash of brown skin and multi-coloured silks, then Aileen was in his arms. *We've made it,* Garamond exulted. *We're all going to live.*

'Is it really you?' Aileen's face was cool and tear-wet against his own. 'Is it really you, Vance?'

'Of course, darling. There's no time to talk now. We've got to get . . .' Garamond's voice was stilled as he made the discovery. 'Where's Christopher?'

Aileen looked at him blankly. 'He's upstairs in his bed. He was asleep . . .'

'But I told you to bring him!'

'Did you? I can't think . . .' Aileen's eyes widened. 'What's wrong?'

'She's gone up there to get Chris. I *told* you to . . .' Voices sounded behind him and Garamond's hunting eyes saw that two guards had followed him almost to the entrance. They had stopped and were looking upwards at the building. Holding Aileen by the wrist, Garamond ran to them and turned. High up within the transparent wall, where Aileen had been a minute earlier, Elizabeth Lindstrom was standing, pearly abdomen pressed against the clear plastic. She stared downwards, screened by reflected clouds, and raised one arm in languorous triumph.

Garamond rounded on the nearest guard and, with a single convulsive movement, snatched the rifle from his shoulder and sent him sprawling. He thumbed the safety catch off, selected maximum power and raised the weapon, just in time to see Elizabeth step backwards away from the wall, into shelter. Garamond's eyes triangulated on his wife's ashen face.

'Is Christopher's room on this side of the building?'

'Yes. I . . .'

'Where is it? Show me the exact place?'

Aileen pointed at a wall section two to the left of where Elizabeth had been standing. The fallen guard got to his feet and came forward with outstretched hands, while his companion stood by uncertainly. Garamond pointed at the power setting on the rifle, showing it to be at the lethal maximum. The guard backed off shaking his head. Garamond raised the weapon again, aimed carefully and squeezed the trigger. The needle-fine laser ray pierced the transparent plastic and, as he swung the rifle, took out an irregular smoking area which tumbled flashing to the ground. A second later, as Garamond had prayed it would, a small pyjama-clad figure appeared at the opening. Christopher Garamond rubbed his eyes, peering sleepily into space. Garamond dropped the rifle and ran forward, waving his arms.

'Jump, Christopher, *jump*!' The sound of his hoarse, frightened voice almost obliterated the thought: *He won't do it; nobody would do it*. 'Come on, son – I'll catch you.'

Christopher drew back his shoulders. A pale shape appeared behind him, grasping. Christopher jumped cleanly through the opening, into sunlit air.

As had happened once before, on a quiet terrace on Earth, Garamond saw the childish figure falling and turning, falling and turning, faster and faster. As had happened once before, he found himself running in a slow-motion nightmare, wading, struggling through molasses-thick tides of air. He sobbed his despair as he lunged forward.

Something solid and incredibly weighty hit him on the upper

chest, tried to smash his arms from their sockets. He went down into dusty grass rolling with the priceless burden locked against his body. From a corner of his eye he saw a flash of laser fire stab downwards and expire harmlessly. Garamond stood up, treasuring the feel of the boy's arms locked around his neck.

'All right, son ?' he whispered. 'All right ?'

Christopher nodded and pressed his face into Garamond's shoulder, clinging like a baby. Garamond estimated he was beyond the effective range of Elizabeth's ring weapons and ran towards the gate without looking back at the Lindstrom Centre. Aileen, who had been standing with her hands over her mouth, ran with him until they had reached the perimeter. The guards, frozen within their kiosk, watched them with uncomprehending eyes. Colbert Mason was standing beside his car holding up a scene recorder. He glanced at a dial on the side of the machine.

'That took two minutes all but fifteen seconds,' he said admiringly, then kissed the recorder ecstatically. 'And it was all good stuff.'

'The best is yet to come,' Garamond assured him, as they crowded into the car.

*

Garamond, made sensitive to the nature of the benevolent trap, never again went far into the interior of Orbitsville.

Not even when Elizabeth Lindstrom had been deposed and removed from all contact with society; not even when the Starflight enterprise had made way for communal transport schemes as natural and all-embracing as the yearly migration of birds to warmer climes; not even when geodesic networks of commerce were stretched across the outer surface of Orbitsville.

He chose to live with his family on the edges of space, from which viewpoint he could best observe, and also forget, that time was drawing to a close for the rest of humanity.

Time is a measurement of change, evolution is a product of competition – concepts which were without meaning or relevance in the context of the Big O. Absolved of the need to fight or flee, to feel hunger or fear, to build or destroy, to hope or to dream, humanity had to cease being human – even though metamorphosis could not take place within a single season.

186

During Garamond's lifetime there was a last flare-up of that special kind of organized activity which, had Man not been drawn like a wasp into the honeypot, might have enabled his descendants to straddle the universe. There was a magical period when, centred on a thousand star-pools, a thousand new nations were born. All of them felt free to develop and flower in their own separate ways, but all were destined to become as one under the influence of Orbitsville's changeless savannahs.

In time even the flickerwing ships ceased to ply the trade lanes between the entrance portals, because there can be no reward for the traveller when departure point cannot be distinguished from destination.

The quietness of the last long Sunday fell over an entire region of space.

Orbitsville had achieved its purpose.

Bob Shaw
Other Days, Other Eyes 35p

Alban Garrod, scientist and amateur detective, creates a new type of
glass which records and stores the events that take place before it –
to reveal these months or years later.

'Slow glass' brings Alban fame, wealth, problems with his love-life
and danger, when the Government, like a super Big Brother, wants to
use micro spy-bugs for its own ends . . .

Tomorrow Lies in Ambush 60p

A crisp collection of eleven thought-provoking stories that combine
original ideas with remarkably real characterization.

The tomorrows lying in ambush involve, among other characters,
a cinema manager who inadvertently conjures up an entire Roman
legion, a bank robber who finds time travel isn't the way to riches,
and a spaceship survivor who undergoes a sex-change . . .

The Two-Timers 25p

Defying time, Jack Breton crosses into a parallel world to regain his
wife Kate, who, nine years earlier, had been found raped and strangled
in a lonely park. In the alternate time-stream, however, Kate is married
to Jack's double, John: for one husband to remain with Kate,
either Jack or John must die . . .

'One of the best time-travel stories I have ever read . . . well-nigh
perfect, with a powerful climax no lover of the genre should miss'
BOOKS AND BOOKMEN

Arthur C. Clarke
Rendezvous with Rama 60p

Rama – a metallic cylinder approaching the Sun at a tremendous
velocity. Rama – first product of an alien civilization to be encountered
by man. Rama – a world of technological marvels and artificial
ecology. What is its purpose in this year 2131? Who is inside it?
And why?

Childhood's End 60p

Blotting out the light from the stars they had linked so effortlessly,
the silent ships hang suspended over the great cities of Earth . . .
Armed with a staggering power and an infinite wisdom, the invaders
from outer space shock Earth into submission – but what is
their purpose?

A Fall of Moondust 60p

The setting – Moon in the 21st century – is depicted vividly and
convincingly. But the vital core of the novel is this: will the crew and
passengers of the Dust-cruiser *Selene*, buried fifteen metres down
in the Sea of Thirst, be rescued before several possible catastrophes
overcome them?

The Deep Range 60p

After a terrifying nightmare in outer space, Walter Franklin needs to
discover a reason for living, and he finds it in the ocean depths,
where strangers defy death to give him life. But Franklin is haunted
by the memory of an echo, an echo that could solve the oldest
mystery of the Sun.

Also available
Earthlight 50p
Profiles of the Future 70p

Robert Sheckley
Options 60p

Tom Mishkin is forced to trek across Harmonia to obtain spare parts for his grounded spaceship.

To protect him from the bizarre and sometimes dangerous collection of creatures on this alien planet there is a Special Purpose Environmental Response robot. Unfortunately, beneath a cynical exterior, his robot buddy is definitely bewildered and something less than competent.

Together they chart a zigzag course from the improbable to the phantasmagoric and beyond...

The Same to You Doubled 35p

The resourceful vacuum cleaner that falls in love with a suburban wife...

A mechanical perimeter guard that nearly kills its controller...

The mild-mannered man who, thanks to the god Thoth-Hermes, need never again be pushed around by authority...

A quintessential collection of sixteen tales to delight and intrigue every SF enthusiast. The time is in the future and the rules of logic are thrown to the wind.

'From the man with the most way-out sense of humour in SF. He can make the most frightening situations seem hilarious and this selection is no exception' YORKSHIRE POST

Mindswap 35p

'Gentleman from Mars, age 43, studious, cultured, wishes to exchange bodies with similarly inclined Earth gentleman; August 1– September 1. References exchanged. Brokers. Protected.'

Exchanging bodies for touristic purposes having become commonplace, Marvin Flynn books a trip to Mars. Once there the unexpected happens and Marvin's mind must seek refuge in a series of temporary bodies on different planets – with some very surprising results...

Theodore Sturgeon
Case and the Dreamer 60p

In Space
No one had been aboard the space ship for over seven hundred years.
It was designed for men like Case – so they brought him back to life.
Mankind had a desire that only Case could fulfil. Luckily, Case and
his computer had a desire that was greater still . . .

On Vexvelt
Why would human beings prefer to die insane and in agony
rather than accept the conventions of this pastoral planet and
its beautiful people ?

On Earth
A dreadful, outrageous idea. But with money no object the only way
to find out whether a thing is impossible is to try it . . .

Theodore Sturgeon 'can handle almost any theme with ease.
Sometimes chilling, sometimes fantastical' SCOTSMAN

You can buy these and other Pan Books from booksellers and
newsagents ; or direct from the following address :
Pan Books, Cavaye Place, London SW10 9PG
Send purchase price plus 15p for the first book and 5p for
each additional book, to allow for postage and packing
Prices quoted are applicable in UK